ADMISSION
LOTTERY

BETTE JOHNSON

Printed in the United States of America
First Printing, 2013

ISBN: 0615779158
ISBN-13: 9780615779157

FOR MAX, JAMES, AND BEN

ACKNOWLEDGMENTS

Many people provided suggestions and feedback to me after reading sections of the narrative at different times or because they were interested in the project. They include Carolyn Mulligan, Alberta Lipson, Bob Emin, Dave Coveney, Bonnie Walters, Roberta Swan, Jean Crichton, Dianne Wylie, Nancy Poe, Gretchen Batra, James Swan, Barbara Vinick, Kip Langello, John Williamson, Mary McMillan, Jerry Burke, Connie Favreau, Julie Parker, Lee Hope, Barbara Tanzer, Reid Williamson, Pat Kasierski, Don Hess, Lisa Dale Jones, Mike Malec, Adam Pachter, Ann Szwarc, Eric Hoffman, Syd Arkowitz, Kate Hoffman, Pam Spagnoli and especially Myrna Malec without whose careful reading, editing, and encouragement I probably would not have finished.

ADMISSION LOTTERY

Cast of Characters

Beacon University
Alan Overton, Professor of Chemistry
Allie Lobelle, Associate Dean of Admissions
Andy, Associate Dean of Admissions
CAFA, Committee on Admissions and Financial Aid
George Kendrick, Director of Resource Development
Jack Bradmore, Assistant Professor of Architecture
James, Assistant Dean of Admissions
Laura Goldton, Dean of Financial Aid
Louise Torrell, alum and volunteer interviewer
Lydia Maroney, Professor of English and Katie's advisor
Maggie, Assistant Dean of Admissions
Marina Dubrova, Professor of Psychology
Marti, Administrative Assistant President's Office
Max Danker, Dean of Admissions
Natalie, Administrative Assistant Admissions
Peter Plank, Professor of Physics
Priscilla Pranek, Associate Dean of Admissions
Charles Skinner, President
Ruth Ann, Katie's freshman roommate
Sue Butler, Graduate student in psychology
Vincent Carr, CAFA chair

Laketon High School
Barbara Lipson, student
Dave, Katie's boyfriend
Katie Lorko, high school senior
Marie MacMillan, guidance counselor
Mr. Rossa, English teacher
Mr. Hoffman, math teacher
Mrs. Ritkowski, writing teacher

Others
Ann Lobelle, Allie's college age daughter
Bill Lobelle, Allie's husband
Bob Vista, Beacon alum and potential donor
Carolyn and Paul Lorko, Katie's parents
Darleen, Max's wife
Paula Kotski, Katie's birth mother
Sofia Solatte, Professor of Architecture at M.I.T.
Nick Carrante, Peter's physicist friend at another college

CHAPTER ONE

Max Danker's navy blazer felt a little too warm for the September day in Cambridge as the fifty-one year old Dean of Admissions crossed the leafy campus of Beacon University en route to President Charles Skinner's house for the annual welcome back party.

Some welcome, he thought to himself. With all the cuts the higher ups have made because of the growing demands on the endowment, how can we get all the applications read in the short time we have? We won't be able to hire graduate student spouses or anyone else. One of my staff, Priscilla, says I need to get tough and require everyone to read at home at least three days a week as well as on weekends. She says I need to hold the line. I hate confrontation. I'd rather choose who to admit by pulling their names out of a hat. Really, how bad could that be? The applicants are almost all good students. On the other hand, if anyone finds out, I'd be in big trouble.

At fifteen minutes past four, Max walked

up the steps of the president's house. The door of the brick mansion opened as if by magic, but actually by an undergraduate in black trousers, white shirt, and red bartender apron who had been standing behind the curtained side panel watching for arriving guests. "Hello. Nametags are on the right." Max glanced at the remaining badges, found his: Maxwell Danker with Dean of Admissions printed below that. He slipped the lanyard over his head.

He stood in the doorway for a few seconds to appreciate the living room with its gold-framed paintings, burgundy Oriental rug, and everyone talking, laughing, and holding wine glasses. The atmosphere appeared wonderfully collegial.

However, he wanted to avoid certain people, especially the Committee on Admissions and Financial Aid (CAFA) members. Who needed questions from the oversight committee at a party? Fortunately, before anyone noticed him, he spotted Marina Dubrova, a faculty member in the psychology department, standing across the room near the punch bowl that he knew from past parties was filled with non-alcoholic punch. She looked good with her long dark hair and the purple dress that hugged her figure. He snatched two glasses of red wine from the tray of a passing waiter, headed in Marina's direction, and handed her a glass.

"Thanks, Max. Ready for it all to start again?"

"I guess. At least all those committee meetings have faded from my memory. I hope you've relaxed. The budget cuts…"

"I'm annoyed," Marina interrupted, "because they reduced the amount I can pay my research subjects. That makes it even more important for me to get the grant I'm working on. They don't seem to cut their own salaries. Nobody is worth that much money. Did you see that article about college presidents' salaries in *The Globe*?"

"I guess we'll all have to make do until the economy improves. The freshmen we admitted last spring have been here less than a month and it's time to start all over again. It's a good thing we love what we do."

"Right," Marina answered. "I don't know how you get through all the applications."

"Even though it's intense, it's cyclical, we know what to expect, and we're pretty careful. We don't make many errors like the one two years ago, when we mistakenly sent someone who hadn't been admitted, an acceptance letter."

"What did you do?"

"We felt we had to take him. He was one of those we could have admitted, but just didn't have space for. I've followed up on his grades and he's done okay."

"That's interesting," Marina said, while glancing around the room. A waiter passing by traded Max's empty glass for a full one.

Feeling even more loquacious, Max continued, "I see Peter Plank over there." At the mention of Peter's name, Max noticed that Marina's attention seemed to refocus. He'd heard a rumor that Marina could not abide Peter, a full professor in the physics department, because Peter had argued against her getting tenure when serving on the university's tenure committee, even though votes were supposed to be confidential. "Last spring at the Committee on Admissions and Financial Aid, the CAFA meeting, he gave a speech about how the freshmen were getting weaker. He's probably lecturing about the decreasing admissions standards, and about the good old days when they used slide rules."

"I'm sure he's telling the same stories he always does," Marina said. "Peter has a fondness for the days when men were men and women were glad of it. Let's get something to eat."

They helped themselves to shrimp cocktail, Brie, and deviled eggs. Max added a slice of roast beef and some Delmonico potatoes to his plate. He followed Marina into the large adjoining library with the comfortable brown leather sofas.

After they'd settled themselves, eaten some of the food, and talked about the weather, Max's twins and his wife Darleen's new job, Marina's new red and black Mini Cooper, and the budget cuts, Max asked, "How's your research going these days?" He knew she was interested in the Pygmalion effect, the psychological concept that she'd once explained to him meant that if the expectations were high for someone, that person would try to rise to the occasion. He remembered her telling him to think of Eliza Doolittle in 'My Fair Lady.'

"Oh, I guess it's okay. My paper on gender differences and the strength of the Pygmalion effect has been accepted for publication in the *Journal of Personality and Social Psychology.* I'm thinking of writing a grant proposal to get funding so I can do the research in a real life setting. We've pretty well shown everything we can with paid sophomores who respond to recruitment efforts to participate in our experiments. I'd like to try it with college students who don't know they're in an experiment."

Hmm, maybe some of Marina's ideas could reduce the time needed to read applications, Max thought. What if they admitted some students randomly? Anyone admitted would do okay if her theory worked. They could collaborate. Before he could say anything, Marina asked, "Do you think I could find a real life study population?"

"I'd like to try something like that with admissions," Max said quietly. "We get so many applicants who are alike. They have good grades and good scores; they all do community service; play an instrument; do a sport. Their essays are fine, but we never know who wrote them, especially with all the helicopter parents out there."

"I just read about helicopter parents, the ones who seem to hover even at a distance.

Do you really think you'd try something like an experiment?"

"I remember reading a newspaper piece maybe in *The New York Times*, in fact I just thought of it the other day about how a lottery would be a fairer system. I'd like to put all the names in a hat, pick the number we need, and that would be that. It would save us having to spend so much time agonizing over every application, trying to make a case where the differences are so small. We make mountains out of molehills. Do you think the Pygmalion effect would work if we admitted students randomly?"

Keeping her voice down, Marina murmured, "I'll have to think about it a little, but I don't see why not. Even if it doesn't work for the research in the grant I'm planning to write, I'm sure I could use the results for a different grant. On the other hand, what if it didn't work as I expect? What if those who were chosen by lottery fail more freshman classes, or decide to leave? You could lose your job."

"If those freshmen didn't do well, that would be a problem, but from what you say that wouldn't happen. Our applicant pool is so strong that most could probably do the work. We would do a quick check to make sure we weren't including in the lottery pool anyone who clearly could not do the work because they had high school grades below B's in major subjects or whose scores were under 500. We can work out those details later." After more sotto voiced conversation interrupted by a trip to the buffet table, Max told Marina he'd meet with President Skinner to find out if he was at least open to the idea of trying some new ways to do admissions. "I'll think about how to broach it before I talk to him. I know my staff wouldn't mind having less reading to do and more free time."

"If you randomly admit some freshmen, and we compare their first year grades with those admitted more traditionally," Marina said, "I might have pilot test data to support my theory."

With that, Max and Marina clinked their glasses, got up, then moved back into the main room where President Skinner was about to give his annual welcome back to campus speech. Knowing it was important to be seen at these events, Max made his way to a spot where he would be more visible.

When the speech was over and everyone felt welcomed, Max took the opportunity to speak to the president. "Hi, Chuck. Nice party. Great food."

"How are things in Admissions? Are you traveling to any fun places this fall?"

"Just the usual. You know it's really not that much fun when the travel is for work. I know you were in Shanghai this summer talking with educators and some alums. That couldn't have been a vacation. Before I forget, I want to tell you about an idea I have to simplify the admission process."

"I can't talk now, but why don't you call

Marti and get on my calendar," he suggested as he patted Max on his shoulder and moved on to a nearby group from the nursing school.

Walking to the parking garage, Max thought about how he would bring up the idea of admitting freshmen randomly. Skinner had a PhD in Experimental Psychology and had published many articles on the stimulus seeking behavior of rats. I know I can't say I plan to select part of the class by putting names in a hat. I can say we need to find a way to save staff time by eliminating careful reads of applicants whose grades and scores are excellent but whose extracurricular achievements may or may not seem special to the committee making the decision. I wonder if he would agree to our not reading all the recommendations and essays? I won't lie, but just present some vague ideas about trying different ways of admitting freshmen, saving time, and especially money.

How can I insure the cooperation of the staff? I suppose it wouldn't be much different from how we keep our deliberations under wraps now. Who should be included? Max thought he'd start with Allie since they'd worked together on other hush hush projects. In addition to Allie, he was pretty certain he could depend on Andy, the publications director. He was always agreeable, especially since Max had increased his salary and title. He thought Maggie, young and single, would appreciate more free time. He knew she liked her job and was looking for good references when she applied to graduate schools. He wasn't sure about Priscilla, the freshman coordinator. She liked to follow the rules and wasn't enthusiastic when exceptions were made. She was also a total workaholic who seemed less bothered than the others by the need to spend seven days a week working during the reading season. If she didn't keep the secret, the experiment couldn't be done. Maybe he could gain her support in a quid pro quo arrangement. He'd suggest she rewrite the Admissions Office manual, a task she'd been asking to do, but one that he'd been unwilling to approve because it would take so much time, and anyway who cared? If Priscilla thought he had decided it was important and she was the one to do it, then maybe she would go along.

CHAPTER TWO

The next day, after they'd both had coffee, Darleen asked Max if he wanted her to pour what was left into his thermos.

"I already have orange juice in it. What's your schedule today?"

"They're doing some electrical work in our area this morning. I'll get there around ten. Don't forget to call your brother back."

"Oh, right. I'll be home around seven." He gave her a hug. "Our summer vacation seems a long time ago already." He still could remember the walks on the beach in Falmouth when they'd talked about her job problems, their finances, and the girls' college expenses, but he felt it wouldn't be long before that vacation seemed a million years ago.

He wished he could forget about calling his brother. Whenever they talked, Max knew he would agree to spend money he didn't have on a vacation to New York City, a dinner at the Capitol Grill, or some concert or other. Darleen had a "thing" with her sister-in-law. She never wanted to admit they shouldn't spend the money, so he couldn't either. He didn't feel competitive with him, though he hadn't thought of buying a Lexus until his brother showed up in a BMW.

Anyway, the Lexus was hardly a luxury. If he was going to spend more than an hour a day on the roundtrip drive to and from Cambridge, he needed a decent car. Darleen, who had done research, said a Lexus was the best one to buy. He turned on the an audio version of a book that his brother had told him about, <u>The Streetsmart Guide to Timing the Stock Market</u>, backed out of the driveway, and waved hello to the next-door neighbor walking her Labrador. He wondered why some people loved their dogs so much. Maybe if I hadn't had all those allergies when I was a kid, I'd have a pet and understand.

He liked the Lexington neighborhood. When Darleen's parents retired to Arizona three years ago, they made it possible for Max and Darleen, their only child, to buy their hundred-year-old house. Otherwise, they'd still be living in a much smaller place. When the girls came home from college on vacations, they all had enough space into which to retreat, even though the heating and property tax bills were high. He thought he could save money this winter by doing his own snow blowing. Last winter he had to pay eighty-five dollars every time the driveway was plowed and that seemed like every week. His father-in-law left the snow blower in the shed, but Max had never used it. He resolved that this winter he would.

By the time he drove into the campus parking garage, he'd listened to a couple of chapters of the book and decided the author's strategy for timing the market was reasonable. He'd give it a try. In the garage, he carefully read the signs to go up on the right, switch to the left, then to the right, and so on. What kind of architect, he thought each time he drove up, would agree to put a garage on such a narrow strip of land? Finally, there was "his" parking space. He felt better when he could park in the same spot every day. He didn't like wandering about, trying to remember where he'd parked. After shutting off the car, he looked in the mirror at his new haircut and felt he looked good especially with the remains of his summer tan.

The garage's damp, oily smell was familiar to him. No one walking toward the exit was. He could avoid chitchat. His brown leather shoes, the sandals of the overweight woman in front of him, and the sneakers of the short man with the Red Sox cap preceding her, echoed in the cement stairwell as they headed down. He thought about the day's agenda: staff members were almost ready to start their fall travel and the budget was going to make everyone's life more difficult than usual.

As Max pushed the office door open, he saw his assistant, Natalie, sitting at her desk wearing a light blue sweater and peering at him over her red-framed glasses. After greeting him, she said, "Before I forget, I picked up the phone without thinking since we're not open yet. It was your wife. She said you didn't answer your cell. She wanted to tell you about an email from her sister-in-law about a big party they're having and not to forget to call your brother. When can we go over your travel schedule so I can make your hotel reservations?"

"I need to do a few things. Can it wait until after lunch?"

"I suppose so. How was the party?"

"Okay. Same as usual. Let's meet at one-thirty." He'd escaped the small talk he hated, but not before seeing Natalie's expression change from pleasure to irritation.

Realizing he couldn't avoid calling his brother, Max decided to do it right away. Maybe no one would answer. After exchanging greetings, his brother said, "My company has a table at a fundraiser for the Boys and Girls Clubs. Can you and Darleen come?"

"When is it? I'm really busy this time of year."

"A little over a month from now, first Saturday in November at the Boston Harbor Hotel, eight to midnight. They usually get some terrific donations. Mark your calendar. I've got to run. Bye." I always go along, Max thought.

What will that cost me? When he and his brother were growing up in Illinois, he was the bigger, older brother who called the shots. It wasn't until his younger brother finished growing and was two inches taller than he was, that the "little" one started getting his way. He's okay, Max thought. He can't help it if he makes a lot of money.

Now, he could take a look at how his stocks were doing. He planned to just take a peek then get back to work. His new stock was down about ten percent. If only I didn't have to pay to get the boat out of the water and stored for the winter. No use worrying, though, something will work out.

Hearing a tap on the door, he closed the computer screen. "Hi, Max. Have you given any more thought to how we'll handle all the reading?" Priscilla said as she sat down across from him and ran her hand through her short black hair that was streaked with gray.

After Max said, "Mmm," Priscilla added that she'd run into the Financial Aid Dean who was worried about the cuts that had been made to the budget. "She wants you to help her make a case that those cuts will hurt the yield. Did you know that some people call her Madame Financial Aid? She's over forty, but she always says she's thirty-nine. Her divorce was final about a month ago. Natalie told me she'd heard gossip linking her with one of the university's big donors. Do you think she really has all those liaisons at the conferences she attends, or is it just malicious fantasy?"

Before Max could respond even if he wanted to, he noticed Allie, his staff's research person, standing in the doorway and pushing her dark brown hair behind her ear. "Hi. I need to talk to you about the data analysis."

Max almost wished he hadn't opted out of an academic career. He'd never thought about how to manage people when he started working in admissions. Many years ago, the Admissions Dean had the locker next to his in the gym at the University of Wisconsin where Max was in the doctoral program in sociology. Responding to his frustrations about being a graduate student, he suggested that Max take a break from his studies and consider working in admissions. A job was open in his office. Max thought if he hadn't left the grad program all those years ago and taken that admissions job, he might be a faculty member somewhere and not have to deal with personnel issues.

After agreeing to talk with Allie later and letting Priscilla vent before she left, he had a chance to open his briefcase and take out the thermos and the manila folders of projects he'd spent time working on at home. He arranged the folders in a row across his desk in piles from least important to crucial. The top priority folder involved the Committee on Admissions and Financial Aid meeting next week. He needed to report on the profile of the freshman class, actual rather than estimated now that they'd arrived on campus. Maybe that's what Allie wanted to talk about. Over the summer, some of the freshmen who had indicated they would enroll in the fall, as Max had expected had "melted" away. The class profile needed to be updated with the actual number, which was almost the same as he'd predicted. Max gave himself a pat on the back for his good planning; estimating the number who would melt was always a tricky business.

On the other hand, the first Committee on Admissions and Financial Aid meeting was usually easy. Peter Plank, the chair, would introduce new committee members; the schedule for future meetings would be announced; and new initiatives proposed. He hoped there would be few initiatives. Mostly they meant more work for his overburdened staff and made little difference to anyone else.

Beyond his office, he could hear the ringing of telephones and Natalie talking with staff and visitors. Natalie's voice had a carrying quality that even through the walls, seemed to pierce the steady drone of everything else. Whenever I feel annoyed by her voice, he thought, I remember that time when she noticed that I hadn't submitted my monthly travel voucher. She saved me from those travel office vigilantes. He realized she also kept overeager alums currying favor at bay. He knew she irritated people, but those same people counted on her for passing along information, given that he wasn't one to indulge in a lot of small talk. I need to encourage her to take advantage of more opportunities for advancement.

"Do you have a minute?" Allie asked Max. "We need to talk about updating the freshman numbers for the CAFA meeting." They talked about the freshman melt for a few minutes.

"I'll have that ready for you by the end of today."

"I have something to talk to you about too," Max said. "You know we have to do more with less this year. I talked with Marina Dubrova, the psychology faculty member, at the party yesterday." Max explained the lottery plan.

Allie looked surprised. "I don't know. I thought 'the match' was really important."

"Well that's what we say, but I don't know if it's true. If we randomly select some from those with good scores and grades who have been selected to receive a full second read, in other words from those who have been triaged in, but where we don't do the full read or carefully evaluate their extras or their recommendations, that is we won't worry about matching their background with our culture, we'd save time."

"Don't you think that would be risky?" Allie asked. "Sometimes in the past when we tried new ways of doing reading, like using students to help and no one outside of the office knew, we had to stop because the students weren't very good at it. When I think back, I'm kind of surprised that Beacon's *Spotlight* didn't have a big exposé that would have made life in the office more difficult."

"You know we've usually been able to keep that and other sensitive things quiet. We'd see how those who enroll from the ones picked in the lottery do fall semester. If they do as well as we expect based on Marina's research, we could do it again and have more time to evaluate the difficult cases."

"Secrets are hard to keep. What if we accidentally admit less academically qualified applicants—that would never fly with the faculty if they found out. State universities use some kind of formula mixing grades and scores, but they expect a greater drop out rate. We have that kind of formula too but we only use it as a guide and we know our pool doesn't have many who are academically unqualified," Allie paused and thought for a minute. "Maybe it's worth a try. On the other hand, it could be a real disaster. Have you talked with any of the other staff yet?"

"I wanted to see what you thought first. I couldn't get an appointment to meet with Skinner until tomorrow. If that goes well, I'll talk to the others. I know there's always the possibility of something going wrong, but I'm confident that with our staff and the quality of the applicant pool, we won't have any problems."

CHAPTER THREE

After talking with Allie, Max thought about the upcoming CAFA meeting. At the last meeting of the spring term, Peter Plank had hurried in to say, "You won't believe what a student in my freshman physics class did. I was lecturing on static equilibrium when a paper airplane sailed toward me. I stopped talking and watched. It flew over the students' heads and I thought it would crash, but it floated to a stop on the table in front of the blackboard, like a pigeon. Whoever launched it had spent a lot of time practicing. If they'd spent more time doing their homework, they'd be better off. When I was a freshman we didn't waste time…." Max remembered thinking, 'not again,' as Peter went on.

He wasn't looking forward to the next meeting and not just because of Peter. He'd become aware of an increase, over the usual steady state, of faculty grumbling about admissions.

Max was about to return a call to a guidance counselor when Natalie appeared at his door. "Max, I'm sorry to interrupt, but

Professor Plank wants to see you." Peter, holding a stack of paper, edged the door more open behind her and waited for a response.

"Hi, Peter. I can see you for a few minutes before my next appointment. Thanks, Natalie." Natalie's eyes rolled up in sympathy.

Instead of sitting down, Peter spread his papers including charts and graphs all over Max's neat desk. He simultaneously said, "I always give a quiz at the end of the third week of classes. Look at these grades. I think the students at the bottom of the distribution have particularly low scores. We need to avoid admitting them," he added, as he aimed his pencil at the bunch of black dots representing grades at the lower end of the chart.

"The first month of classes isn't even over," Max protested. "Maybe they'll get better?"

"I've taught the course enough to know that those who score low on the first test will have a hard time all the way through. I think they're students who have low SAT math scores."

Max started to interrupt, but Peter continued, "You're going to say I shouldn't focus on SAT scores. When I saw some of the answers they wrote on the quiz, I tried to figure out why. Maybe the quiz was too hard, but I don't think so."

"Why is it the scores?"

Max suspected that Peter probably asked the lower scoring students about their high school records and learned their SAT scores weren't the highest.

Instead, Peter said, "I know you believe scores aren't that important, so I want to do a study. I'd like to look at the relationship between SAT scores when they apply and grades in freshman physics or chemistry courses. If I'm wrong, and lower math scores aren't related to bad grades, I'll stop talking about them. But if I'm right, we should start looking more carefully at the scores before we admit students." Max believed that Peter's great faith in a strong relationship between scores and how well one did in college was based on his own experience. He'd been told that Peter, as a high school student, had scored eight hundreds on his tests.

Max sighed and thought why can't he want to teach better? No, it's easier to blame the scores and want only those students most prepared to do physics or chemistry, but all he said was, "What kind of study do you have in mind? The data from the College Board place our freshmen among the best anywhere."

What Max didn't say and what Peter seemed to suspect, was that not all students who were admitted had top scores. On the other hand, Max never allowed anyone to be admitted who had no chance of succeeding. His ethical, or was it his survival, sense wouldn't allow that. Diversity was the key. Some of the freshmen were good lacrosse players, others top notch cellists, some had parents who were neurosurgeons or stockbrokers, others had parents who were migrant workers, but all of the students Max and his staff admitted had the potential to be good enough, if they wanted to be. If they also liked to enjoy themselves and have fun with their friends, that gave the campus life. Peter probably didn't share his opinion, he thought.

Max knew that President Skinner did support his strategy, at least the part about increasing diversity on campus. The president, with his training in psychology, believed that given the right teaching and encouragement, even those with less than perfect educational backgrounds could be strong achievers both at college and in today's multi-cultural world.

Max and Chuck Skinner shared idealistic and practical goals. Both wanted to be part of a university that turned out alumni accomplished in the humanities, adept at science, and financially successful enough to be reliable donors to the university, aspects of data that would contribute to obtaining even higher ratings in *US News and World Report*. Those ratings were important both for admissions and for the president.

Max felt comfortable with Skinner's major social goal of recruiting students from high schools not traditionally oriented toward colleges like Beacon. As educators who earlier were influenced by an academic culture that encouraged everyone to consider the benefits to all of diversity, Max Danker and Chuck Skinner loved the idea of finding diamonds in the rough. One of Max's goals was to find people like Paul Farmer whose biography he'd read in Mountains Beyond Mountains. He wished he could admit people like Paul who had experienced an unconventional childhood, was admitted by Duke, went on to medical school, and followed that with an amazing career as a founder of Partners in Health.

Max was brought back to the present when Peter said, "You know I think you and your staff do a fantastic job. The majority of freshmen are exactly what we want. Unfortunately, there are more than a few who don't measure up. I hope you and I can find a way to avoid these mistakes in the future."

"What about the freshmen who are enrolled? Do you think anything would make them better? Can Beacon's Center for Teaching help? Remember how your department improved physics understanding by teaching in small groups rather than in large lecture classes?" Max guessed that Peter didn't like anyone telling him how to improve his teaching any more than Max liked being told how to do his job.

"I'll have to deal with the way they are. I'm more concerned with figuring out why they were admitted in the first place and having you use that information to avoid admitting more of that type in the future."

"You know, the Admissions Office has to be a broker for the university. We want to admit students who'll be turned on by your physics class, but we also need people to play in the orchestra and do theatre. The hockey coach just called and put in a plea for more goalies. Someone in fund raising wants me to check the credentials of the sons and daughters of potential donors." Max noticed that Peter's eyes had glazed over when extracurricular activities were mentioned.

"Look, I need to see the high school data," Peter said. "Give me the admissions applications so I can understand why they were admitted. I'm really busy, but I'll read old applications of a hundred students who enrolled at least four years ago. I know we can't look at students who haven't finished their science requirement; we'd get into trouble. You can select those who've finished the requirement. Blank out all the identifying information and I'll write down my opinion as to whether they would be good students in physics or chemistry, or the type who'll have real problems. Now that all freshmen have to take some kind of lab science, it's important to be sure they have the ability."

That's all I need Max thought, while saying, "I think that will be a lot of work for you. There's a good chance you won't find anything to differentiate the ones who don't do well from the rest."

"I've already talked to Alan Overton from the chemistry department and asked him to read the applications too and give his opinion. We'll see if we can come up with some guidelines to help the Admissions Office make better decisions," Peter said then walked out the door.

Max took a deep breath and thought I guess Allie can organize the old applications and delete identifying information. Could Peter be right? Were the students not as good as they used to be?

Back at his desk, Max thought he'd like a drink. In past years, he'd kept a bottle of sherry in the back of his closet and would have a glass if he had to stay for a dinner meeting. After Natalie made her nose twitching remark last year about how "It smells like a bar in here," Max decided to change his drink from something that could be detected to one that could not. If he had to stay for a late meeting, he'd add some vodka to his thermos of orange juice. Today, he didn't have an evening meeting nor did he have anything but orange juice in his thermos. He didn't abuse alcohol, just used it to relax, like a glass of wine before dinner. Right now he was stressed by the complaints coming from faculty, by his bad investments, and by the need to manage his decreasing office budget. He worried about the image his failings would project. He could talk to his wife, and did, but she had recently changed jobs and was trying to find her way in a new setting. His old friends in the Midwest were still there, but over time they were less frequently in contact. For whatever reason, he felt he didn't have the same kind of relationships at work as he'd had in his previous job. Most of the faculty seemed too busy teaching their classes, doing research, and trying to publish. He believed if he were a little more social, he could find people he enjoyed, just as he believed he could stop calling up his stocks five times a day to see if his retirement prospects had improved. He just needed to do it.

"Hi, Max. Mind if I come in?"

Max looked around to see Alan Overton, slightly overweight and smiling. "Oh. Hi, Alan. I'm guessing Peter talked to you. He was here this morning and told me he'd spoken to you about some detective work he wants to do," Max said. "He thinks we admit the wrong students. What do you think?"

"There are always a few who aren't up to par, but whenever I've talked with them, I learn they aren't putting in enough time, or something else is involved, like a roommate, girlfriend, or parent. I don't have a lot of time to spend on Peter's project, but just between you and me, I agreed at least in part because I'm applying for a summer research stipend and Peter's on the committee that makes the awards. Peter made it clear he wasn't happy with his class and asked what I thought of the freshmen. He's okay but he sometimes comes across pretty strong. For instance, he said some mother called him to say her son was having trouble and she hoped Peter could help."

"I hope he was tactful," Max said.

"He was more gracious than I might have expected. He's worried the freshmen aren't as good as they used to be and that the wrong types are admitted. He mentioned an email he got from some academic friend at another university who found out a student of his was rejected by us even though he'd scored eight hundreds on his SAT's. Peter feels there's virtually no faculty input into admissions decisions. He said something like, 'When Borden Brown was the dean, you could count on him to make good decisions. I hoped Max would be okay, but now I'm concerned.' I'm not telling you this to make you feel bad, but I think you should know what he's saying. I'll try to be fair in my involvement in the project. Like I said, my students are not that different from the way they've always been. I have an appointment in about ten minutes, so I have to get going. I know there are some faculty who find it easy to blame the Admissions Office for all their problems. Peter might get some support. I'll do my best to tamp it down. Let me know what else I can do," Alan added as he left.

Later, the phone rang. When he picked it up, Natalie said, "Max, Peter Plank is on the line. He's gotten another professor to agree to read old applications to see if they can predict who will and who won't do well in the science courses. Is that something you know about? Should I tell him you're going to follow through?"

"Yes, I guess I can't avoid it."

"Is there anything I can help you with?"

"Do you ever hear anything from staff or

students about how we're admitting the wrong people?"

"There's always some of that. Do you think it's worse than usual?"

"I guess not, but I want to make sure I'm not missing something that everyone else is talking about."

"I've been your assistant for four years, and I've worked for college administrators for the past twenty. There's always a lot of support for someone new that gradually falls away. Some people think this place is more about criticism than praise. Remember that former dean of students who left in the middle of the night? You're not going to wind up like him are you?"

"No. I like my job. Sometimes, though, it's hard to recall why. I realize faculty want students who are good in their classes; they don't have a reason to care if students are active in extra-curricular activities, unlike us in admissions who can use that as a marketing point in recruiting prospective applicants."

At home that night, Max told Darleen about Peter's experiment and also about Alan's visit.

"You're right," Darleen replied, "that faculty expectations and needs are not the same as those of people who have to deal more with the world outside of the university. I've met Peter a few times at parties and found him charming in kind of an old fashioned way. I remember he insisted on getting me a napkin when I didn't have one at the cocktail party for that Nobel Prize winner. Have you tried to see it from his point of view—I mean what it's like to try to teach physics to those who are not well prepared? Some high schools don't do as good a job as others. Maybe the experiment Peter wants to do will help him see that it's not the scores, or you'll see that Admissions should pay more attention to them."

"You sound like you think he's right. We don't deliberately try to annoy the faculty. We know they are important along with the president and the trustees. Allie will get him the old applications he wants to look at and he and Alan can do their experiment. It probably will be a waste of time, particularly for Allie, but we know we have to go along. There is the chance, however unlikely, that they'll find something useful." He hoped that Peter would be proven wrong.

CHAPTER FOUR

At work the next day, Max was about to call Darleen when the phone rang. Natalie's voice explained that an alum, Bob Vista, wanted to speak to him about some new high school in California. "Do you know anything more about him?" Max asked.

"I've never heard of him, but he seems all enthusiastic about whatever it is he wants to talk about."

"I'm really busy, but put him through."

"Hi, Max. You probably don't remember meeting me at the reception for alums in Northern California a couple of years ago. You told me you had twins who were thinking of going to college on the West Coast."

"I do remember. You worked for a computer start up. My twins enrolled at Stanford."

"That's great! Now, I'm retired. I'm calling about a new private high school out here, Gateway Collegiate, which a few of us who made money in the high tech field, started. Our goal was to offer a curriculum geared to those who want to study tech subjects in college. I'm a trustee."

"Sounds good."

"Is it crazy to hope that you would admit more than one student from any particular school? Some parents at Gateway are worried that their kids will be competing for the same spot."

"We admit as many students from a high school as we think can do the work and who will add to the mix."

"That's what I hoped to hear. Another part of my story is that I've had a call from George Kendrick in Donor Relations. He's got me thinking about making a large donation to Beacon. But let me cut to the chase. I want to offer you the chance not only to provide me some help with the new high school, but also an opportunity to make a little extra money."

Max wondered if Bob was on the level. What was his idea of a large contribution? "I'm glad you think enough of your education to plan on making a donation. What exactly do you have in mind that I can help you with?"

"You're such a good speaker. Parents are interested in learning as much as they can about how admissions works. You should hear the questions they have of the college counselor. I want you to come out here and talk to them. I'll guarantee that my friends involved with other private high schools will invite you to speak at their schools, too."

"If I can work it into my schedule, I'll be happy to do that."

"One of your staff that I talked with at the

college night last year, said that your applicant pool is so strong that many, or even most, of the students you reject could have been admitted. Given that, I'm sure our juniors, who will be the first graduating class from Gateway next year, will be just as admissible as anyone. My business experience has made me realize the importance of the personal connection and that's why I'm calling. I know Beacon will pay for your expenses to come out here, but I'll make sure the honorariums you're given from each school total around ten thousand dollars. How does that sound to you?"

Before he responded, Max found himself wondering whether Bob was asking him to do something unethical. Was this a conflict of interest? For the moment, he decided to go along and later reconsider taking the money. "I appreciate your thinking that I'm good enough to draw the attention of parents at your school and at others in the area, but you may be overestimating my appeal."

"I've heard enough from people who've been at your talks to know that you're a draw."

"I think it's important to explain the admissions process to parents, so I'll be happy to accept your invitation, if we can find time in my schedule that works for both of us. I'll tell Natalie, my assistant, to expect a call from you about a date for me to come to California."

"It'll be a boost for our school to get a few

of our first graduating class admitted to a place of Beacon's caliber."

After he hung up, Max wondered if they expected him to admit, not one, but two, or even more students from that new school, what was the name, Gates, no Gateway. He never said he would admit anyone, at least he didn't think so. He would have to clarify that point with Bob. On the other hand, it was true that many applicants were admissible, and if Bob did make a big donation and also enabled Max to make a little extra money, there seemed little harm in being positively disposed to applicants from Gateway Collegiate. It didn't mean he'd have to admit anyone. That would depend on whether there were any admissible applicants.

While Max was still trying to figure out exactly what he'd agreed to, he heard his door open.

"I hope I'm not disturbing you," Laura Goldton, the Dean of Financial Aid, said as she closed the door behind her. "I need to talk to you about the possibility that the trustees may have to increase the amount of loan our next freshman class will be expected to assume."

"I did hear something about that."

"The decline in the market a few years ago reduced the endowment, and that continues to affect our ability to subsidize the tuition we charge. If we can't subsidize as much, students will have to borrow more. Donor Relations has been trying hard to get some large gifts from people who agree to have their money go toward financial aid rather than for the more visible naming of buildings."

"I heard some rumblings about the stock market affecting our ability to be as generous with financial aid as in the past," Max said and thought about Bob Vista's recent proposition.

"I was over at Donor Relations yesterday afternoon when George Kendrick was talking with a potential donor from California who is one of our alums. He's made a zillion dollars in Silicone Valley. George did an excellent job of getting him to think about making a large donation for financial aid rather than for a structure with his name on it. He's also interested in admissions, so I thought I'd stop by and let you know in case George, or even this guy, gives you a call. I realize you admissions people don't let yourselves be influenced by outsiders in your decisions, and I don't think you should, but all things being equal, this is one of those situations where anything that will get this guy's money into the financial aid pool may be worth the cost. Well maybe not anything, but you know what I mean."

"Admissions has a pretty long tradition of avoiding influence about whom to admit. I'd hate to see that change, but I get your point," Max said to Laura before she left.

What a day, Max thought. When I came in, I was trying to figure out how to tell Darleen we need to cut expenses. Then Bob materializes out of thin air and wants to help his alma mater, and for whatever reason, me too. Kind of a quid pro quo, but nothing illegal, Max equivocated, as he punched Natalie's extension number. "Natalie, if that alum, Bob Vista, calls to try and find a time when I can go out to California and give some speeches, do your best to arrange it, even if you have to cancel some things already on my schedule."

There was a light tap on his door that opened to frame James, the minority recruiter. "Can I talk to you for a minute?" Without waiting for Max to say yes or no, James walked over to the couch, lowered his tall, lanky frame and sat down. "I'm really bummed. I just talked to Jerry, my counterpart in financial aid. He says that he's taking a new job and that his financial skills translate into a lot more pay than he receives here. I know when Denise left this office and went to work for the business school in Donor Relations, she got a big salary increase. I suppose I'm telling you things you already know, but it's frustrating. I mean I like my job, but for all the time I spend doing it, I wish it paid more."

Max did understand, but didn't know exactly how to help. "Some of these things are just the way everything works. I'm not sure what we can do about it, at least in the short run. All of us feel overworked and underpaid. Do you have any suggestions that I could use going forward?"

"I don't know. I'm just annoyed because with my kids needing all kinds of stuff—you wouldn't believe how much sneakers cost—the budget is really tight and I have so much to do in this job. In the long run, I suppose I can find something that pays more. I like my job, but I'm not happy that others similar to myself can make more money."

"Wait until your kids are in college. It seems like the tight budget never ends no matter how much money you make. I guess none of us can expect to get rich working in an academic setting." In the back of his mind, Max was considering whether the Dean of Financial Aid earned more money than he did.

"Thanks for letting me vent."

Max wondered if something was going on in outer space to cause the week to be so affected by money issues. Just yesterday his brother had called to brag about all the money he'd received from stock options at his company. Max told himself to think seriously about Bob Vista's offer.

When he walked into the kitchen that night, he found Darleen setting the table. "Can I help?"

"You can make a salad. I've got potatoes in the oven and the salmon is ready to cook. I really wanted to go out, or at least get take out, but everything is so expensive. Maybe I should look for some additional part-time physical therapy jobs. I'm scheduled so tight, though, that I can hardly think straight. Most of the clients are okay, but today I had this guy who hurt his leg running. He calls a lot to ask when he can start running again. He doesn't want to take any painkillers, even ibuprofen, but wants me to give him more exercises. I tried to explain that healing takes time and that he's doing what he should, except for taking the anti-inflammatory pills that would probably speed up the healing. Some days I wonder if I'm in the right field," Darleen added as she cut up a lemon after pushing her blond hair behind her ears.

"Maybe after you've been in the job longer, you'll have more time and can look for some consulting because you're right about us needing the income. We need to follow through on the financial issues we talked about at the beach last summer. If the twins weren't in college, we wouldn't have to be so careful. But they are. We have to watch our expenses."

"I know," Darleen said. "Even with the loans we receive, it's pretty tight. I probably shouldn't have quit my physical therapy job at the hospital to take one at the gym, but I needed a change from working with people with disease caused problems to working with people who have exercise related injuries. At the time I didn't know the gym would cut my hours to three days a week. I do like the work better. We're not in the top one percent, but even so you'd think we could live on your salary alone. In this area it's not enough with the girls in college."

"I'm glad you like your work better

though. My job is okay even if each year is kind of a repeat of the last one. We'll have to be more careful, but we'll manage." He knew he'd have to be more cautious about his stock investments. "By the way, I had a call today from an alum being cultivated by donor relations." Max told Darleen about the call from Bob Vista, the visit from the Dean of Financial Aid, and his conversation with James who felt underpaid. "I didn't tell Laura I'd just talked to Bob Vista. I know it's not unusual for some Admissions Offices to be influenced about acting favorably toward certain candidates, but we've been above all that. With more needy students, maybe it's a new era. I don't know what to think," Max said as he washed the lettuce and waited to hear Darleen's opinion.

"About the alum who wants to provide you with a large stipend for doing what you do, I think you have to be careful not to encourage a belief that Admissions has a price. I think you'd be on pretty shaky ground accepting that much for something that's part of your job. I know we could use the money, but we can figure out other ways to reduce our spending. I don't think you should take that kind of money. I think you should give the talks, but only for the usual honorarium. On the other hand, I suppose if the candidates are pretty equally qualified, then who would know why you admitted one and not another."

Max and Darleen debated the pros and

cons back and forth for a while before turning on the television to watch the news while they ate their dinners. "Do you remember that story awhile ago about a large state university receiving criticism for giving preferential treatment to children of large donors?" Darleen asked. Max did remember. His mind also flashed back to a story about financial aid deans who were involved with moneylenders. They'd lost their jobs. He knew he didn't want to wind up like that.

CHAPTER FIVE

Walking across campus toward the president's office, Max wondered whether he should say they needed to try different strategies each of the next few years, admitting a small subset of freshmen in untraditional ways to see if any staff time and, by implication, money was saved. How could he get an agreement for the lottery plan that he knew he shouldn't exactly mention? Inside, precisely at nine forty-five, Marti came out of an inner office and said, "Max, President Skinner will see you now."

He and Marti exchanged pleasantries about the weather as she ushered him in, closing the door and leaving the two men alone.

"Hi, Max. I only have a few minutes; so let's get right down to business. What can I do for you?" he asked as he moved to sit on the sofa across from Max who was already seated in a leather chair on the other side of the coffee table.

"I think you know that the number of freshman applicants keeps increasing and...."

President Skinner interrupted, "The number of applications we're receiving has been very impressive. The trustees think you and your staff do a spectacular job. In fact, I was just talking to George Kendrick in Donor Relations this morning. He has some alum in California who is very impressed with you. George hopes to turn his interest into a large donation."

"Thanks," Max said, thinking to himself, that alum certainly has made an impact. "I appreciate your comments. But the growth in admissions numbers is both a blessing and a curse. Our staff hasn't grown to match the increase in applications that need to be read. I'm not here to push for more staff, though. I know money's tight. What if we admit some academically qualified freshmen in a way that takes less staff time, then follow up later to see if their grades are similar to those admitted the traditional way, that is, by carefully reading their essays, recommendations, finding the right matches for the Beacon culture, and ..."

President Skinner interrupted with, "Exactly what do you mean?"

"We get many applicants who have top grades, top scores, and seem to be good citizens. Often they don't stand out in our pool of fantastic candidates. They have the academic skills to do well here; we don't have enough space to admit all of those who are qualified. From those that a staff person selects to be given a full read, what we call triaged in, we could admit some without looking closely at their extracurricular activities or essays and follow up to see how they do. In other words they would be similar to those who do get a full read from whom the committee admits only a small portion. They should have good study skills and do okay. If we didn't have to pay attention to their extracurricular activities and essays, we could save reader time and use it to do more careful reviews of those considered desirable to have on campus, like the first generation kids who attend less competitive high schools, or those the coaches would love but who we're not sure can handle the academics. I feel we get so pressured to get through all the reading, we aren't able to really understand some of the more complicated cases."

"You know I'm interested in leveling the playing field for the less advantaged, but I don't know. Tell me more."

"So, we would do a basic screen to eliminate applicants with grades lower than B in major subjects. We could also make sure that anyone selected had no suspensions so that we wouldn't be putting ourselves at too much risk." Max could feel his heart beating a little faster.

"I'm not sure. I can hear the faculty, especially if they were to find out by reading the *Spotlight's* headline, 'STAFF EXPERIMENTS WITH ADMITTING FRESHMEN!' On the other hand, as an experimental psychologist I like the idea of using that approach with a small group and then carefully evaluating the results."

"I think some of the faculty would like it if we paid less attention to the extracurricular activities," Max said as Peter Plank's name almost reached his lips. "I've been told the grades and scores are what they think most important." There was a knock on the door. Marti stuck her head in to announce that the alum founder of Zoo World was waiting.

"I have to meet with this person," Chuck said. "Can I give you a call in about an hour so that we can talk more?"

"I'll be there. Thanks."

When he came into the admissions reception area, Max tried to sneak by and get to his office without being seen, but as usual he was noticed.

"Max, your wife called to say you're not answering your cell phone and she needs to talk to you, and you received a FedEx letter," Natalie said.

Who would send a FedEx letter? Max wondered. He pulled out the letter and learned that a Mr. Rosty, the father of an applicant, wanted to be sure the Dean of Admissions was aware of what a perfect human being his son was. A copy of his son Russ's resume was attached. Max wrote "file app" on it and added a sticky with Priscilla's initials, 'PP', at the top with a note asking her to reply. That's all I need, he thought, individual letters from parents. What are they thinking? When had the application process become such a family event?

When he went to college, he applied to

two schools in Illinois, one where his father was a professor. He would have been happy to attend either. Now applicants were applying to ten, fifteen, even twenty colleges, partly because the Common Application made it so easy. What a waste of time, he thought. Rather than doing the hard work before applying, they looked in detail at the colleges after they were admitted. Oh well, he reasoned, at least it means more application fees for us.

When President Skinner called, they discussed the project in more detail, including Marina Dubrova's involvement, and finally decided to admit four hundred, given about half of whom they estimated would enroll. "We usually expect the yield, that is, the percentage of admits who actually enroll, to be about fifty percent," Max said. "In addition to the four hundred we admit this new way, we'll accept another sixteen hundred the traditional way, for a total of two thousand admits. Eight hundred and two hundred will give us the one thousand we want to enroll."

Max hoped his staff would feel the experiment was an opportunity to try something interesting. He knew they could be hung up on doing things the way they always had. Admissions people were notorious for being afraid to change anything, in case that would result in fewer admitted students enrolling. Even more importantly, he didn't relish the idea of seeing a story about the special admits plastered on the front page of

Beacon's *Spotlight* or even worse, *The Herald,* or *The Boston Globe.* On the other hand, the office had been good about keeping past questionable projects quiet.

He called Marina to tell her Skinner was okay with the plan. They would accept four hundred special admits with the expectation that two hundred would enroll. Marina began to sputter that she wanted a larger sample, but Max interrupted to say it was the best he could do. Marina decided she could work with it. They made plans to meet the following week to discuss the details.

CHAPTER SIX

After his brief talk with Marina about President Skinner's approval of their project, Max told Andy about the plan. "I like the idea of finding out if the match is important," Andy said. "Why DO we bother evaluating all the non-academic aspects of applicants?"

"We do it because we think students who are a good match for Beacon, in terms of their essays, recommendations, and interests, will do better if they want to be in this kind of environment," Max said. "Even though you'd think students who apply here would know what we're about, I'm not sure that's completely true. Kids are applying to so many colleges, they often don't bother to figure out which ones are best for them until after they've been admitted."

"I guess we do all the reading to make educated guesses about who will and who won't do well and who has the energy to both do the academic work and get involved in activities," Andy said.

"Sometimes it's hard to know if we do

things because they really matter or if we do them because that's what we've always done. Anyway, this experiment might help us figure out how important it is to read in detail all the information the applicant sends us. I've already talked with Allie. We'll find out what the rest of the staff thinks about the project when we get together this afternoon."

By five minutes past two, Priscilla, Maggie, Andy, James, and Allie had arrived in Max's office for the special meeting.

Before Max had a chance to start the meeting, Allie asked, "Does anyone else overhear mothers, in all kinds of places, talking about their children's college application process?" Everyone nodded. "I was at the hairdresser's when I heard a woman in the next chair say that she was exhausted because she and her husband and their high school junior had just returned from a driving trip to visit colleges. They loved the campus at Princeton. She went on and on about how beautiful the buildings were, yada, yada, yada."

"I hear them too. I guess it's exciting for the whole family," Priscilla added. "I feel like an undercover agent when some person near me talks on and on about one college or another and how wonderful it would be for her son or daughter. I have to hold back from stepping in and offering my opinion."

Max interrupted to say, "I have something important to discuss that we need to keep under wraps. If we don't handle it right, our jobs could be in jeopardy, or at least our relationship with the administration and faculty could be affected. You're all aware of how much time we spend reading applications. I'm going to talk about a way we can cut that down so that we can spend more time with complicated cases. You know the budget is tight and we aren't able to hire more readers. Marina Dubrova, a professor in the psychology department is going to work with us on a special project. Marina's hypothesis is that if people think they're special, they act special. She's done experiments using college students. She'd like to do the research with people who don't know they're part of a study. That's where we come in. I talked with Chuck Skinner yesterday, although I didn't exactly go into details. He supports a plan in which we admit a small portion of the class without carefully reading their essays, recommendations, and evaluating their interests. Marina expects those admitted this different way will do just as well as those whose records we examine more carefully."

"Wait a minute, are you telling us that we'd admit anyone off the street?" Priscilla asked.

"Yeah, that would work. I can just see them in Peter Plank's course. They'd last about five minutes and be out of here and so would we," Maggie added.

Max went on to explain how the experiment would work, how those selected at random would be similar to those who received a full second read, etc.

"I don't know, I'm worried there will be a higher failure rate in the subjects freshmen are required to take if we don't read all the supporting information including the essays," Priscilla complained.

Maggie looked at her with disbelief. "I don't look forward to spending every weekend from November through February trapped by applications if it isn't necessary."

"As long as the students we admit have good grades and scores, I don't think many of the faculty will care," Allie said. "On the other hand, sometimes things we don't think will be problems for anyone in the university become major issues that we have to spend lots of time trying to minimize. I'm not sure the time we would save would be worth it."

"In the past, we've talked about how significant involvement in extra or co-curricular activities along with good grades insures that our freshmen have the energy level to handle college life and get good grades. This will let us evaluate whether that match between their style and Beacon's is important," Andy said.

"Skinner said he would provide funding for extra support services for all freshmen, no matter how they were admitted," Max said. "Those who need help will be able to get it."

"I don't know. I don't like the idea of doing something that has to be a secret. I can't believe that it won't get out," Priscilla grumbled.

The discussion went on for about ten

minutes, or until Priscilla was convinced that the experiment was not likely to result in students being admitted who were much different from those admitted the traditional way.

After the meeting ended, Maggie asked Max if he was interested in participating in a group purchase of megabucks tickets. She and Natalie were organizing an office pool. They'd heard admissions staff in another state won the major lottery prize and quit their jobs. "Even though we all love our work, wouldn't it be great not to have to, but do whatever, sort of like being retired without being old?" Max gave Maggie a dollar. Allie, who was standing nearby, told her she'd get a dollar from her pocketbook when she returned to her office. "I'm glad that we may not have to spend as much time reading," Maggie said to Max. "I just want a normal life. If someone calls and wants to go out, I'm either too tired or I'm behind and can't go. I don't know how long I can keep up this lifestyle and actually have a life."

"Are you still dating that guy, what's his name, Jesse?" Allie asked.

"No, he moved to New York."

"How about your plan to go to graduate school?" Max asked.

"I need to fill out applications, and I don't have time."

Max shook his head, said he had to make a phone call and they left.

Priscilla came back into Max's office.

"How will we pick the lucky four hundred? Will we put all the names of those who are selected for a full read into a hat?"

"I think we can iron out the details later. If this works, we might be able to save time. If the data show that the special admits are as successful as the regular ones, in the future we might decide to use some version of the random admissions plan to admit a larger percentage of the class. Then we'd have more time for those we'd like to admit, but don't have time to evaluate thoroughly. For now, we're talking about a small number of cases admitted this special way."

"Maybe for this project we should restrict the special admits to high schools with only one applicant. How many applicants are the only ones from their high schools to apply, do you think?

"I'm not sure, but I think it's quite a few," Max said.

"That way the guidance counselors at the high school level won't see anything funny," Priscilla said. "Whatever we can do to make it less likely anyone will find out, the better. On the other hand, it makes me nervous when we have to do something secretly. What if Peter Plank or someone else on the oversight committee finds out?"

"That wouldn't be good, but Skinner is supportive," Max said. "I guess if he's willing to take some of the responsibility, we should be okay. By the way, I've been thinking about that rewrite of the Admissions Office manual you wanted to do. I think you should do it."

"I'll get started on it as soon as I can," Priscilla said. "Why do you think Skinner agreed? I guess if you've been trained as a psychologist like he has, you're always looking for ways to explain behavior. I have to get back to my office and answer all the emails. Have you gotten the one from the kid with fifty specific questions about how students are admitted? I'm going to tell him to look at our web site for the answers," Priscilla said as she left.

Max shut the door and turned to his computer. He checked his email and answered the one from President Skinner's office about the date for sending out decisions. He went to his bookmarked web sites and called up his stock portfolio. He was anxious to know how the market was doing.

Even though he didn't have immediate money problems, he knew he would have to borrow to pay the twins' tuition when the bill arrived. When we bought the Cape house, I assumed stock and house values would keep going up, he thought. With Darleen's job we earn almost $200,000. I don't know why we can't save more.

The stocks were doing okay today. The meeting with the staff had gone fine. Even though some objections were raised, all the staff finally agreed that the experiment was worth a try. If everything went as well as Marina expected, in the future, I won't need to request more staff. I might even earn a name as someone in the vanguard of college admissions.

CHAPTER SEVEN

Bill kissed her goodbye, then Allie stepped up into the van in front of her house and a half hour later was dropped off at the airport for the late morning flight to Chicago. On the plane, she reviewed her notes for the evening's meeting. She thought about the recent conversation she'd had with Max. The lottery plan seemed risky, what with all the attention the office got from faculty, prospective students, and their parents. On the other hand, the idea of doing an experiment to find out if their assumptions about the importance of finding the "right match," were correct was intriguing. Bill thinks it's a great opportunity even though he admits there's a chance it won't work out as Max or Marina expect.

At O'Hare, she picked up the rental car, drove to a hotel in the Loop, unpacked, and had a quick meal in the coffee shop. By six thirty, she was at the high school prepared to hold that night's meeting. The Beacon alum, a pediatrician, who was in charge of coordinating the alum interviewers for the area's applicants, arrived about the same time carrying an impressive array of snacks, including bottles of water, juice, cookies, crackers, and chips. High school students and parents waited attentively and expectantly. One father, sitting next to his son who was wearing a Boston Red Sox sweatshirt, looked bored. He's probably been to a few other college meetings this month, she thought.

After the alum introduced Allie, she told the audience that she would talk for about forty minutes, then take questions. "First let me hand out a quiz."

Heads went up. A few smiled. A nervous, "A quiz?" was heard from a mother in the second row.

YOUR FIRST BEACON QUIZ

1. Beacon's motto is:
a) Mens et Manus
b) Pax et Lux
c) Veritas
d) Ever to Excel
e) Learning, Virtue, Piety

2. Which of the following can you study at Beacon (check as many as apply):
a) Physics
b) Music
c) Engineering
d) Philosophy
e) Management
f) Math
g) Architecture
h) Psychology
i) Economics
j) Volleyball

3. Beacon's graduation rate is approximately
a) 10%
b) 50%
c) 60%
d) 91%
e) 100%

4. What percentage of Beacon's freshmen return for their sophomore year?
a) 10%
b) 35%
c) 68%
d) 82%
e) 97%

5. How many undergraduate and graduate students participate in intramural sports?
a) Less than 100
b) 400
c) 500-600
d) Around 4,000
e) Around 9,000

6. How many varsity sports teams does Beacon have this year?
a) 12
b) 22
c) 33
d) 94

7. Approximately what percentage of Beacon's undergraduates are women?
a) None, Beacon is only for men
b) 50%, by quota half must be
c) 100%, women have taken over the world
d) 45%

8. A competitive SAT-I Math Score is around:
a) 800
b) 700
c) 600
d) 500
e) 450

9. UROP is an acronym for:
a) Useless Requirement, Obsolete Preparation
b) U Really Oughta Prepare
c) Undergraduate Research Opportunities Program
d) Underwear Required on Premises

10. A "Hack" at Beacon is:
a) a taxi
b) a police car on top of the dome
c) a weather balloon eruption at the Harvard-Yale football game
d) a bean-bag ball juggled with the feet
e) a nagging cough during a physics lecture

11. T or F: Only people who wear eyeglasses are admitted to Beacon.

12. T or F: Only football players get athletic scholarships at Beacon.

13. T or F: Beacon offers only need-based financial aid.

14. T or F: Beacon's Early Action deadline is November 1.

15. T or F: Beacon's mascot is the elephant.

16. T or F: You can get both a Bachelors and Masters degree in engineering in five years at Beacon.

Answers:
1. a   2. all but j   3. d   4. e
5. d   6. c   7. d   8. b   9. c
10. b & c   11. F   12. F; no merit aid is offered
13. T   14. T   15. F   16. T

"I find it easier to get through a lot of information using the quiz. I'll read the question. You pick the answer from the listed choices." For the next half hour, the audience learned that Beacon's mascot was the beaver, as well as other more useful information: scores are important in the admissions process, but high scores won't necessarily assure admittance; what a competitive score is; how applicants are evaluated for what they will add to the mix of students.

Allie was struck by what she'd just said. If Max's lottery plan worked, maybe in the future they wouldn't care about the match or even the mix, maybe decisions would be made only on the basis of grades and scores; maybe the lottery wasn't such a good idea.

Someone else asked if interviews are important. "Interviews are required but an interview will be waived if there isn't an interviewer who lives in the area. More applicants who have interviews are admitted."

Another student asked about how important senior year grades were for admissions. Allie said fall semester senior grades were very important to maintain as good or better than those from previous semesters. Grades going down seventh semester could negatively affect admissions chances.

A young man with narrow rectangular black glasses kept darting his hand up and down to get her attention. She motioned for him to speak. "What are the average SAT scores you need to get in?"

Allie gave the SAT score means for a recently admitted class while thinking, why is it always the SAT scores? I guess it's because it's easier for students to think about how to improve their scores than how to improve their grades or leadership skills or how to stand out in the pool. Not long afterward she said, "Well our time's up. I'll be happy to stay around for any individual questions you have. Thank you for taking the time to come tonight. I hope to see you all in Cambridge."

The audience applauded politely. Immediately a dozen students and parents came toward the front of the room.

A mother lowered her voice to say, "We have a special situation. I didn't want to ask it in front of everyone. Rob had a hard time in English last year. The teacher is well known for having favorites. He got a D. Will that hurt his chances of being admitted? Should we explain what the teacher is really like?"

What a stupid question, Allie thought. Instead of saying of course it will hurt your son's chances of being admitted, she said, "Grades are important. An occasional C can be okay, but a D isn't good. There can be a valid reason for doing poorly and an explanation can help."

The father and the son in the Red Sox sweatshirt were next. Mr. Hunter introduced himself. The younger Hunter said, "I've been to a few other college meetings where the admissions person said it was important to say on your application that the college you're applying to is your first choice. Is that true?"

"It's important to make it clear why you're applying. It certainly doesn't hurt to say it's your first choice, but we have no way of knowing whether that's true or not. On the other hand, if you give some reasons why you want to attend that show you know what we're all about, that makes a better case."

Mr. Hunter asked, "Why should someone like my son, who is a really good student, President of the Student Council, on the math and soccer teams, consider Beacon? He'll be eligible for a full scholarship at the University of Illinois where I went, and he can get a top education there according to *US News and World Report*. Why should we spend so much more money, even borrow it, for Will to go to Beacon? I know you have a top reputation, but it costs a lot more money."

"The opportunity to attend is one that only a few people get. Beacon is a brand name standing for smart, creative people, but every family has to weigh whether it's worth the higher cost and financial choices. When you apply, you can also apply for financial aid."

"But doesn't applying for aid reduce your admission chances?" Mr. Hunter asked.

"In Admissions, we don't know if you're a financial aid applicant. If you are admitted, you will receive a separate financial aid package. You'll know how much aid you'll receive before you decide whether or not to enroll."

"So you really don't know who is an aid applicant?"

"Not at Beacon. One reason to enroll, I think, is that Beacon students achieve more of their academic potential at least partly because academics are the name of the game. No one is embarrassed to have to work hard; it's almost a badge of honor to announce how little you slept because you had to finish your math homework. That same persistence and high ability to achieve are valued by graduate schools and employers; a Beacon degree can open doors."

Mr. Hunter took out a business card from his case and handed it to Allie; at the same time, he gave her a warm, somewhat prolonged handshake, and said, "We plan to visit in a few weeks. Can we look you up when we're on campus in case we have any questions?"

"Just come to the Admissions Office and ask for me." Allie went on to encourage them to take the campus tour and attend the information session when they were on campus. She noticed there were still about ten students and parents waiting to talk to her. She took another drink of water. The next student asked, "Is it better to take a higher level English class that I might get a B in, or take one where I can easily get an A?"

"The quick answer is it's better to take the higher level course and get an A. You should take the course that best meets your needs. Taking or doing something just because you think it will help you get into a college can be a waste of time, especially if you're not admitted. If your high school is one from which a low percentage of students go on to four year colleges, then you should be getting mostly A's; however, if your school sends a lot of students to four year colleges, then we'd view the high school as more competitive and regard B's as acceptable."

A man and woman were next. The woman explained, "Our son had a conflict tonight, so we've come as his representatives. I've had a hard time setting up the interview for him. I called the person whose name was on the website, but he hasn't called me back. What should I do?"

"Some interviewers are quicker to respond if the applicant himself calls, so you could have your son call and see if he gets a better response. If not, and a couple of days pass, contact our office, tell them what you've told me, and ask them to give you a different interviewer."

Next, a young woman said, "I'm Barbara Lipson. My guidance counselor asked me to find out if you could visit Lexton High School tomorrow."

"Unfortunately, I have to drive to Indianapolis. Is there anything I can help you with tonight?"

"Ms. MacMillan, my guidance counselor, said your admissions representatives never visit. She thinks you only go to private high schools."

Some of the fun of the job is the chance to do things that might surprise people and make them happy Allie thought. "Tell you what. If I change my plans and come to your school tomorrow morning around nine, will that work?"

"I know Ms. MacMillan will meet with you, and I can get my history teacher, Mr. Hoffman, to let you talk to his class."

"Okay. Sounds like a plan. I'll call your school tomorrow morning. You'll have to talk to Ms. MacMillan and Mr. Hoffman as soon as you get there."

Next a young man in a blue blazer, khaki pants, and striped tie asked if they ever admitted students younger than fifteen. "Are you asking for yourself?"

His mother, standing behind him, answered, "Yes. Johnny's thirteen and very ready for college. He's taking courses at the local community college and attended summer classes at Northwestern. He's very interested in Beacon and we want to know if he'd be considered for entry next fall."

"We sometimes admit students who are younger or who are not in their senior year of high school. Besides taking college classes, what else do you do with your time?"

"I play tennis with a community club and the organ at church and sometimes at nursing homes and I've just finished the requirements for Eagle Scout. I've also started doing research with one of the physics professors at the community college. We're working on string theory."

Johnny's mother added, "He has a very busy schedule and he's well rounded. That's important we think."

"Why do you want to leave high school?" Allie asked.

"I want to do research at the college level."

"We're cautious about admitting students under fifteen. College is more than classes, research, and activities. You'd be expected to live in a dorm, unless you were able to live near the university with a close relative. Younger students may be better off attending college closer to home. If you want to talk more about this, call me when I'm back on campus next week. I can put you in touch with some students who enrolled when they were younger. "

I'm ambivalent about younger applicants, Allie thought. On the one hand, I understand the difficulty of being more advanced academically than peers. On the other hand, some younger and academically advanced students are not well developed socially. Thrusting them into a milieu in which sex, alcohol, and sometimes other drugs are easily available with no parental supervision seems risky. Parents sometimes forget that aspect of college. We'll have to eliminate younger applicants from the lottery if we get to that.

It was time to pack up and then figure out how to get back to the hotel. The laptop computer was in her travel bag; the leftover brochures, quizzes, and other materials were now in the cardboard box. The alum had collected all the leftover snacks and carried them out. One final look around, nothing was out of place. After putting on her black jacket, adding her pocket book to her shoulder, and positioning the travel bag on top of the cardboard box, Allie picked the box up and walked out of the empty room into the corridor leading to the front door of the building. She could see the rental car, a subcompact green Hyundai with Ohio plates, ahead of her all alone in the visitors' parking lot. She'd trained herself to note the make, color, and state of the license plate ever since that time in Wichita when with a few hours before her flight, she'd stopped at a shopping mall and been unable to find her car when it was time to head for the airport.

She vaguely remembered entering a store and walking through the men's shirt department. The car keys only had the license plate number and state of registration, Kansas, on the tag. She'd spent about twenty minutes walking around the parking lot growing more and more anxious about missing her flight. She noticed a mall security car riding though the area and was on the verge of flagging it down when she saw the license plate she was looking for on a Taurus. With no time to spare, she got into the car, but missed her flight. The next one to Kansas City was an hour later. She arrived five minutes late for the start of that evening's meeting. She vowed never again to forget where she had parked.

After she put all her boxes and bags of admissions material down on the ground, popped the trunk, put everything in, and slid behind the wheel, she took out the address of the Chicago hotel where she had checked in earlier. The drive would take about forty-five minutes in the dark.

This year she had a rental car with a GPS and knew she would avoid the anxious kind of drive she'd once had in California. She'd left a meeting site in darkness like tonight. She knew the hotel was in San Jose and entered the freeway going south. After driving for about fifty minutes, she realized she must have missed the exit because the huge highway sign listed Los Angeles as well as some other city that was not San Jose. She got off at the next exit, that turned out to be a lonely long ramp into a state park, not the type of place she wanted to be by herself in the dark. She turned the car around just as the headlights of another car approached. She accelerated toward the highway this time driving in the reverse direction. Fifteen minutes later, she came to the San Jose exits. Although she enjoyed the opportunity to meet prospective applicants, getting lost, and being late, usually because of being lost, were aspects of travel that were not fun.

The GPS directed her onto Lakeshore Drive. After winding her way back to East Ontario and the Midwestern Hotel in the Loop, she parked in the nearby garage. She dropped the evening's registration materials onto the bed and called Bill. "Hi. I just got back from my meeting in Evanston. It's a nice night here. I think I'll take a walk up Michigan Avenue toward the Water Tower. What's new with you?" After they talked for a while, she hung up, put on her sneakers, took the elevator to the lobby, and walked out of the hotel. She needed time to decompress. Even though she would have to get up at six tomorrow morning in order to get ready and be at Lexton High School at nine after driving in rush hour traffic, she knew she wouldn't be able to get to sleep right away.

The autumn night was perfect with its full moon. Many other people seemed to be out enjoying the evening on Michigan Avenue. Allie looked in the windows of the stores. She wished she could return in the morning to take a closer look at a particularly nice sweater. Chicago had many memories for her. She'd been in graduate school at Northwestern. While there, Paula, her best high school friend, told her she was pregnant and planned to give the baby up for adoption. For a few months Paula had lived with her aunt in one of Chicago's suburbs. Allie was with her when the baby was born. She wondered where that baby, now a teenager, was.

Back at the hotel, Allie wrote her meeting report. She listed the types of questions she'd been asked, rated the meeting site for next year's traveler, and checked her office voicemail. A mother and daughter who had attended a previous meeting in Minneapolis planned to visit Boston and wanted to know if she would be there. After that, Allie watched CNN, ate a Snickers bar, and shut off the lights.

The next morning as soon as the radio alarm went off, she got out of bed and checked the weather. The sun was not yet up. She turned the television to a local station. The temperature was on the screen: fifty-nine degrees. The weather person said the day would be sunny. At least the drive to the high school and later to Indianapolis would be in good weather. In the Burger King near the hotel, Allie ordered orange juice and a sausage biscuit and coffee.

Back in her room, she called Lexton High School and spoke with Ms. MacMillan, then checked out of the hotel, picked up the car, and drove west to the Dan Ryan. Thirty minutes later she looked for visitors' parking spaces in front of the high school.

Inside, students were walking through the halls, some wearing cheerleader uniforms because it was "spirit day." In the guidance office, an attractive dark haired woman came over and said, "Hi, I'm Marie MacMillan. After you meet with Mr. Hoffman's class, you can look over the file we have for Beacon material that we've received in the past. Let's walk down to the class." They joined the throngs of students headed in both directions through the hall.

Allie liked the energy and exuberance she

felt in a high school when classes changed. A bell rang. The noise and chaos ended. Except for the sound of doors closing, the hall was once again silent except for the heels of the two women tapping on the highly polished floor.

Ms. MacMillan knocked on the classroom door and then opened it. The twenty students sitting at movable desks arranged in a semi-circle looked up. Mr. Hoffman greeted both women.

"When Barbara told me she'd arranged for you to visit, I was pleased because I graduated from Beacon some years ago and enjoy getting updated about the campus."

"If you don't mind, I'll stay for part of your presentation," Ms. MacMillan added.

"Before we start, let me introduce Mr. Rossa one of our English teachers," Mr. Hoffman said.

"I asked to listen because I have a couple of students for whom your college might be a good choice," Mr. Rossa said. "They have an AP calculus test this period and couldn't come."

"I'm glad you were able to take the time," Allie said. "Shall I start?"

"Yes, go ahead. The period ends at 9:55," Mr. Hoffman replied.

"I'm very happy to have a chance to speak to you today about Beacon University. Were any of you besides Barbara at our meeting last night?"

A dark haired young man with glasses

raised his hand. Mr. Hoffman quickly said, "That's Bobby Chen."

"Hi, Bobby. Let me know if you have any questions that weren't answered last night."

"My cousin Bing who lives in China wants to know if the requirements are the same for applicants who are not U.S. citizens," Bobby asked.

"Beacon has an freshman quota for foreign citizens who are not permanent residents of the U.S. The quota is ten percent of the enrolling class. The important thing to know is that not all colleges are the same with regard to entrance requirements for foreign citizens. Some colleges are happy to accept all those they think can do the work, without regard to their citizenship status. Have any of you been to Boston?" Two students raised their hands.

"Here's a map that shows where Cambridge is located relative to Boston. We're north and west of the city center. I like to tell people that if Washington is government and New York is finance, Boston is college. Does anyone have a question?"

"I do. How much does it cost to go there? My parents think I should go to a public university because it's less expensive," a girl in a cheerleader uniform asked.

"We're a private university and the cost isn't subsidized by taxpayers in the state as it is at public universities. The price will be higher than the state university's, but all students are eligible for need based financial aid. Need is calculated from the information your parents submit about their income and from their tax return for the past year. You need to fill out the federal form for financial aid, the FAFSA. The average aid award is around $25,000 a year. That means the average family is paying around $15,000. You can tell your parents to look at our web site for more details."

"I have a question," Ms. MacMillan said. "What kinds of applicants are most likely to be admitted?"

Allie gave the same answer as the night before.

After leaving Mr. Hoffman's class, she walked back to the Guidance Office and looked through Beacon's file where she found different versions of various publications. The same recruitment pieces for 2008 through last year were there. She tossed them all into the recycle basket and inserted information about the website and the brief 'how to apply' brochure. She added some information sheets about athletics and financial aid. "I've updated the file," Allie told the office assistant. "Is there anything else you need me to do before I leave for Indiana?"

"No, that's it. Have a good trip. Thanks for visiting."

As Allie drove out of the parking lot and onto the interstate, she had the thought she sometimes had since reading David Lodge's book, Trading Places, in which two academics going on sabbatical to each other's universities are on flights that cross each other over the Atlantic. She imagined admissions officers from different colleges driving their rental cars, passing her as they headed in the other direction, everyone worried about getting lost, being late, or forgetting their credit card at the place they'd just left.

After she was on the highway, Allie turned on the radio and scanned for the local NPR station. She heard her cell phone ring in the bottom of her pocketbook. When she stopped for a break on the four-hour trip, she'd check to see who'd called.

At that moment, a huge bug splattered on her windshield and that made her think about her recruitment trip several years earlier when she'd been traveling in South Carolina. The hotel room's toilet malfunctioned. Allie was moved to a new room nearby. She forgot her robe hanging behind the bathroom door, but recovered it the next morning. Unknown to her, a roach, probably the same one she'd seen on a glass door leading out of her floor to the outside, had made it's way to the robe and then to the inside of her suitcase and been transported to North Carolina. At dinner with local alums, she felt a zissing sensation on her stomach. In the ladies room she found the bug inside her half slip. Now, years later, she could calmly remember the event, but also could still remember the anxiety she'd felt that night. Who knew what might have happened during the meeting in front of a hundred people if the bug had still been inside her slip.

Recruitment travel was almost always interesting, Allie thought, as she entered the parking lot of the rest area. She rummaged in her pocketbook for her phone wondering if Max had rethought the experiment, of if Peter Plank wanted more applications, or if her daughter wanted to talk to her.

After returning from her recruitment trip, Allie thought about the question Mr. Hunter had asked at the Chicago meeting: was it worth the extra money to send his son to Beacon? She thought it was worth it, and for some especially low to middle income families, the cost might not be that different from the cost of lower priced colleges once need-based scholarships were awarded. "Worth it" was not a simple economic question, she thought, although maybe that was a place to start. Some time ago, she'd seen an article in *The New York Times* about executive pay[1]. She googled the names of the highest paid thirty executives named in the article to find out where they'd gone to college.

When she was looking at the results, Maggie came into her office. "Do you get asked whether it's worth paying more for a Beacon degree?" Allie asked Maggie.

---

[1] "Executive Pay: A rich year, and more to come," April 10, 2011, p. B 7.

"I get that question at most of my recruitment meetings. Unless you're a multimillionaire, it's hard not to be concerned about the cost, especially if you have more than one child."

"I get the question too. When I came back to the office, I remembered seeing some story in *The New York Times* about top paid executives and wondered where they'd gone to college so I looked them up on the web. I just finished compiling the results. The college name is followed by whether they are private or public."

Colleges of Top Paid Executives

Boston College, private

City College of New York, public

Dartmouth College, private

Ithaca College, private

Johns Hopkins University, private

New York University, private

Northern Michigan University, public

Quinnipiac University, private

Saint Cloud State University, public

Slippery Rock University, public

Stanford University, private

University of California-Berkeley, public

University of Central Oklahoma, public

University of Florida (2), public

University of Illinois, public

University of Kansas, public

University of Pennsylvania, private

University of Texas, public

West Virginia University, public

Yale University, private

"I counted and there are only twenty colleges listed. I thought you said thirty?" Maggie said.

"That's right. Of the thirty, nine of the executives were educated outside of the United States and one more, Lawrence Ellison, chief executive of Oracle, didn't finish a bachelor's degree but started college at the University of Illinois. The others graduated from twenty universities including eleven publics. The nine private colleges are much smaller than the publics so I called someone I know at one of the college associations and was told that private not for profit colleges award only between one fourth and one third of all undergraduate degrees. So even though there are fewer top compensated executives who went to small colleges, someone could argue that the privates are overrepresented in the group of colleges producing top compensated executives. Beacon wasn't on the list this time anyway."

"Earning potential isn't the only reason to go to a particular college," Maggie said.

"I know. It probably isn't the best measure of college success, just easier to measure than personal qualities such as happiness. I guess it's worth knowing that no one college has a corner on producing the highest paid executives or that the list is limited to only the most selective universities."

CHAPTER EIGHT

"I've been thinking about how we'll do the research," Marina said to Max after they'd exchanged telephone greetings. "I'm still annoyed that Skinner wouldn't agree to more random admits. Four hundred is okay, but it's a minimum."

"I hoped we could admit a thousand, half of all the admits," Max said, "but we'll have to be satisfied with fewer."

"Maybe I should talk with him. Does he know I'm involved?"

"Yes, I thought your involvement would help sell the project, and even though he didn't agree to as many as we wanted, it helped. He said he knew your research, that you had a bright future ahead of you. He's a social scientist like you, and also like you, he's interested in extending lab research into real life settings. Are four hundred admits really not enough?"

"Well I'd rather have more, but assuming half of them will enroll, two hundred will be adequate to see if the random admits are different from those chosen more selectively."

"There won't be much to do until these random admits enroll next fall," Max said. "Then we'll have to wait until they finish the first semester and maybe even the second semester."

"Before I talked with you at the welcome back party, I was trying to write a grant proposal to fund my Pygmalion, self-fulfilling prophecy, research," Marina said. "Maybe I told you that. I was enthusiastic about the proposed study, but in my head I kept hearing the voice of my thesis chair telling me to find ways to do research in situations occurring naturally. The grant proposal I was working on would use students paid to participate in a lab setting, one mimicking real life. However, the opportunity to team up with the Admissions Office, behind the scenes, and to analyze the data about how the students admitted randomly actually do, is much more exciting. I even fantasize about getting a phone call from the MacArthur Foundation a few years from now. My parents would be so proud and Peter Plank so jealous.

"I don't think we should get too carried away," Max said while thinking that her enthusiasm might make her less vigilant about the risks of this project.

Marina told Max that she was a good example of the way the Pygmalion effect worked. Her parents, immigrants to the United States from the old Soviet Union, had high school educations. She was an only child, born a year after her parents arrived in New

York, a studious type, but had not been otherwise special. In high school, the guidance counselor, Gail, had taken a special interest in her. In addition to working full time as a guidance counselor, Gail was taking courses toward a doctoral degree. As part of her training, she had to pick a few academically talented students whose confidence needed boosting and keep detailed notes of weekly meetings with them. "I was one of the students selected. You should have seen me. I was a shy, scared freshman." Marina went on to say that because of the confidence building, she'd been elected treasurer of her junior class, and as a result, became an excellent prospect for top colleges. Later, when she was a college senior, she was admitted to one of the best social psychology graduate programs. "Now I have tenure and my research is devoted to finding ways to facilitate individuals becoming the best they can be."

"Very nice. Do you mind if I just run through what I think we're going to do?" Max asked while thinking spare me your life details. "We'll accept four hundred freshmen randomly from a pool of all those applicants selected for a full second read. This experiment will tell us if we need to do those careful second reads that take so much time."

"What is the point of the second read? It seems that the person doing the triaging in or out can tell from the quick look he or she does who has the right stuff?" Marina asked.

"The second read fills out the picture. The

applicants give us a short list of their special talents, yet sometimes after reading the folder what seemed special on first glance, seems less interesting. The person who does the full read tells us that as well as other things that are buried in the essays or in the teacher, guidance counselor, and interviewer reports."

Max and Marina discussed how she'd compare the end of semester records of the random admits with those admitted the traditional way to learn whether her theories of Pygmalion type behavior were supported in a real life situation.

Marina said she had a graduate student, Sue Butler, who needed a topic for her dissertation; the special admit study might be perfect for her. Sue could collect grade and other data from the Registrar for the study and do the analyses. Later, she could follow the students during their sophomore year and find something to analyze for her dissertation. "I feel she's the right assistant for this study. Whenever I've seen her with others, she seems pretty quiet. She should be able to keep the details of the research under wraps until it's finished. I'll make a note to talk to her."

"Maybe you should make up a story to tell Sue. Tell her that Admissions plans to send different letters to this year's admitted students to see if the letters affect how the students perform once they enroll," Max said. "At least it would lay the groundwork for all the contacts and permissions we'll need. You don't have to tell her the real reason for the research."

"The Admissions Office would have to send different letters, and then we'd have to rule out the letters having some affect. In order to evaluate whether the two groups are different because of the way they're selected, we can't have any other so-called 'treatments' that might make a difference. No," Marina said, "I think she's trustworthy and competent. We don't need to confuse what we're doing. I'll get her started."

Sue Butler was sitting at her desk in the graduate assistants' office eating, when a voice behind her said, "Hi, Sue. Do you have time to talk for a few minutes about a research project I might get involved in?"

Sue turned, swallowed the banana in her mouth, and said, "Hi, Marina. Sure. Do you want to talk here?"

"Let's go to my office. Bring your food." She headed out the door followed by Sue carrying the banana and a laptop. Sue locked the office door. After a series of thefts had occurred on the third floor, Sue and the other graduate students with space there agreed to keep the room locked.

She followed Marina into her office and sat down at the black conference table, opened her laptop, peeled the rest of the banana, and ate it. Meanwhile Marina put away her class material, grabbed her Starbucks coffee mug, asked Sue if she wanted something, and went out the door. She returned within a minute with her mug filled with tea and sat down opposite Sue at the table. "Here's what I want to talk to you about. I might have a chance to do some real life research that's related to the Pygmalion effect. It won't happen until next January and won't be finished until next June, but in the meantime, I'd like you to set up a spreadsheet and a timeline so that we'll be ready." She told Sue that some of next fall's freshman class would be admitted differently from the rest, with less emphasis, for example, on extracurricular activities. After the freshmen finished fall semester, she wanted Sue to examine whether there were any differences between the two groups for grades and other measurable items.

"Do you want me to talk to the Registrar's Office about this so that we'll know what we need to give them to get the grade data?" Sue asked.

"Yes, that's a good idea. If they need forms filled out, do that. I don't want you to tell anyone the nature of the study, though. Some people might be nosy. Just say we need to look at freshman grades. We'll tell them who to put into each group, but we don't need to know which person goes with which grade, so we won't be violating any privacy rule, I don't think." Sue had a few minor questions and then left. As she walked back to her own office, she saw Monica walking toward her.

"We're heading over to the Brown and Brew. Want to come?" Monica asked.

"I have so much work, I shouldn't."

"We're only going for half an hour. We're all really busy. Come on. You need a break."

"Okay. Let me drop off my stuff." She rejoined Monica, Tom, and Sonam, and they all walked over to the union. Two hours and many cups of coffee later, Sue returned to work hard to make up for the lost time. Back at her office, she named Marina's research folder that was on her computer desktop, "work," just in case anyone was snooping. Next week she would think about how to proceed with the project. There wasn't any rush. Right now she had to finish grading last week's quiz from Marina's Theories of Personality class. The students would expect to get the tests back tomorrow. It was a good thing she'd stayed until ten-thirty last night. All she had to do now was record the grades and make out the grade distribution chart. She received a text from Monica telling her they were going out for Indian food because Sonam needed her fix. Did she want to come? Sue negotiated a time when she felt she would be done with the grading. When she finished, she sent Marina an email with the grade spreadsheet attached, packed her backpack with her laptop and cell phone, locked the door, and left to join the others near the elevator.

CHAPTER NINE

When the class ended Mr. Rossa asked Katie, "Can I see you for a minute?"

Have I forgotten to pass something in, Katie wondered? She grabbed her backpack and walked up to Mr. Rossa's desk. She waited until Eric finished asking his question.

"Thanks, Mr. Rossa. Hey Katie, going to the concert tonight?"

"If I finish my newspaper article. How about you?"

"My sister's in it. I have to go."

Katie had known Eric since junior high when she was cast as Fiona in the eighth grade production of Brigadoon and he was in the chorus. Katie ran her fingers through her strawberry blond hair that hung loose. She wished she had a hair band to pull it up with. "You wanted to see me, Mr. Rossa?"

"I have something to give you. A Beacon representative talked to Mr. Hoffman's class yesterday and I sat in. She said to give this information about their website to students we think might be good matches. I thought of you."

"My parents want me to stay close to home and U of I is less expensive. Isn't Beacon in Massachusetts and hard to get into?"

"You know I have a ten-year-old daughter, and I understand how your parents feel. But if she becomes as good a student as you, I want her to think about all the colleges where she'll be challenged and excel. I went to U of I, enjoyed it, and did well, so I'm not saying you shouldn't go there. Just think about some other places. Beacon is expensive, but there is substantial need-based financial aid. One of my English professors at Illinois took a job there and we've stayed in touch. From what he's told me, you're the sort of student they want. Read the material on their website and think about it," he said as he handed her the information.

"I'm not sure it's worth all the time it would take to fill out the application. Why should I bother with a college that probably won't admit me anyway?" Katie asked though she was flattered that Mr. Rossa thought she should apply to a college of Beacon's reputation.

"Just take a look. It's one of the best schools in the country for English. If you want me to talk to your parents, I will."

If she stayed any longer, she'd be late for writing class, so Katie put the material into her backpack. "Thanks," she said hurrying out the door as the next period bell sounded. Mrs. Ritkowski handed back papers as Katie quickly took a seat toward the back of the room. In spite of what she'd said to Mr. Rossa, she was excited about the possibility of attending a college like Beacon. She knew she was the apple of her parents' eyes; they'd do anything for her, probably even let her go a thousand miles away, if that's what she wanted.

But she didn't know what she wanted. She'd spent a weekend in Urbana and enjoyed the parties and the people at the University of Illinois. Even though she thought she'd appreciate the independence of college, she liked the idea of being within a few hours of home.

Mrs. Ritkowski said that instead of working on their college essays, she wanted to use the period for a discussion of their concerns about where to apply. "Katie, how about you?"

"When I started thinking about college I decided I wanted to stay close to home. I couldn't imagine living more than two hours away. But now I'm wondering if I should be less concerned about distance."

"Have any of the rest of you thought about the pro's and con's of going to a college close to or far from home?" Mrs. Ritkowski asked.

Eric raised his hand, "I have. My father thinks I should go to U of I. He says it's one of the best engineering schools in the country according to some ratings and it costs a lot less than MIT or Caltech."

"Those are good points: cost and

reputation. How many of you have read some college guide book?" Almost all twenty of the seniors in the AP English class raised their hands. Someone said he regularly read the website College Confidential.

"You can get a good education just about anywhere, but campuses have different personalities, or cultures, or what I like to call 'feeling tones.' Some will be better matches for you. I know from my son's experience that many of the most expensive colleges also have the best financial aid. His top two choices were U of I and Stanford. Even though Stanford was more expensive, there was good financial aid. Mr. Ritkowski and I pay more to send him there, but we don't pay the 'sticker price,' you know, like when you buy a car, the full cost. Your parents fill out forms explaining their situation to the college and often you'll get financial aid to cover some of the price. If my son had stayed closer to home and gone to U of I, we'd be able to take fancier vacations, but he's met people and had opportunities he probably wouldn't have had in Urbana. We're both teachers and felt it was worth the money. Apply to your dream school even if you think it's expensive."

The bell rang.

"For Monday, pick one of the essays for a college where you're considering applying, and write a draft."

Katie felt excited about looking at Beacon's application on the web and figuring out if she wanted to apply. She wondered what her parents would think. Sometimes Katie imagined what her life would be like, if instead of having been given up for adoption, she'd grown up with her birth mother and father. She knew it was crazy to speculate about something so unreal. She'd been told she was adopted as soon as she'd been old enough to understand. She'd learned more about her birth mother, Paula Kotski, when Paula died in a car crash a few years ago. Katie's mother's cousin, Jane, who'd been involved with her adoption, heard about Paula's death and talked with Katie's mom. Her parents told her about the death so she wouldn't wonder why Paula never contacted her. For Katie it was a disappointment to know they would never meet. At the same time, she felt she couldn't ask for better parents, even if they were a little over protective. She was an only child and sometimes wished she had a sister to talk to, but most of the time she was happy as she was.

Walking home from school after tennis practice, she started to think about how she would talk to her parents. She shut off the music playing on her iPod, hoping the silence would help her think more clearly. She knew they'd be pleased that Mr. Rossa felt she should apply to a college of Beacon's caliber. But her parents would want to know why she would consider going that far away from home. She was afraid they would think that a major reason she wanted to go to college in Massachusetts was because her birth mother had grown up there. Although that was a part she admitted to herself, she also had dreams of a life beyond her present borders. Chicago was a great city, but she didn't want to spend her whole life in Illinois. She could always come back, but college was the chance to try new things. Her boyfriend, Dave, was planning to go to U of I. She 'really really' liked him and was worried that if they went to different schools, they'd break up. She wasn't sure she would ever find anyone she liked as much, but neither of them was willing to commit to a permanent relationship. Why did Mr. Rossa have to give her that information about Beacon? Now she would probably apply. If she went there, what would happen to her relationship with Dave? And if she went to U of I would she always feel she missed something?

When she got home, she left the Beacon website information on the dining room table, the place where all mail got sorted. If she put it there, her mom would probably notice and say something.

Katie's mom came home from work around five thirty. "Hi. How come you're doing your homework in the kitchen?"

"I'm reading an article for AP history and it was easier here."

Her mom put away the groceries she'd picked up on her way home. Katie took the plates and silverware from the cabinet and set the table. Her mom took the chicken and pasta casserole out of the refrigerator where it had been defrosting, turned the oven on, and put the casserole in to heat. The day was a little cool and having the oven on would make the kitchen feel warmer. Her mom took out the salad fixings, put all the ingredients into the wooden bowl, and then placed the bowl in the refrigerator.

With all the supper preparations started, Katie watched her mom go into the dining room to look through the mail. She could hear her sorting through it. She waited, and then heard her mom ask, "Katie, do you know anything about this Beacon University information?"

Katie got up from the table and moved to stand in the doorway. "Yes. Mr. Rossa gave it to me and said I should look at the website. He sort of thinks I should apply."

"Does he think we're rich? It's a good school, but we can't afford the cost."

"I told him you wouldn't want me to apply."

"I didn't say that. Why did he give it to you?"

"He heard a talk by a person from Beacon who gave him information to give to students he thought should apply. He thinks it would be a good place for me."

"Isn't it awfully hard to get into?" her mom asked, but Katie could hear that she was pleased.

"That's what I said, but he told me the

Admissions person made him think I was the kind of student they're looking for. They have good financial aid."

"Mr. Rossa said that? I know you're a top student and you do all those other things, but I thought you'd already decided to go to U of I?"

"I kind of have. But he said to take the material, look at the website, and talk with you and Dad. He said you could talk to him, too."

"Do you want to go that far away from home?"

"Not really, but it wouldn't be forever. Boston seemed like a nice place when we were there with Dad for his meeting. I loved the Swan Boats. It wouldn't be any colder than here and Boston's not that far, at least not as far as California. I don't know what to do. I decided to apply only to U of I and now I'm all mixed up. I was afraid maybe Mr. Rossa would be disappointed if I told him I didn't want to look over the information. What do you think I should do?"

"Why don't we wait until your dad gets home? We can talk some more then. I have to check the oven."

Katie followed her and the smell of cooking chicken into the kitchen. She sat down at the table and pushed her plate out of the way so she could open her laptop and find the admissions website. The questions on the first page seemed pretty straightforward: parents' names and places they'd gone to college. Uh oh. Were Mom and Dad "really" her parents? She was adopted. Should she say anything about that? How would she explain it all? They even wanted to know if her parents were married. Why do they care? Would they think she was less qualified because neither had graduated from a university? She didn't want to make her mom feel bad about that so she'd ask Mrs. Ritkowski what she thought. Even these ordinary questions seemed kind of tricky if you weren't the typical applicant. Maybe she shouldn't apply. It was certainly easier to send an application to U of I. However, Mr. Rossa was so nice and he wanted her to apply. The application asked about brothers and sisters. No problem there, except maybe they'd think she was a selfish only child.

Then there was a question about her favorite activity and why. She liked all the things she did, but she liked acting the best. It gave her a chance to pretend. When she was little, she liked playing make believe with her friend who lived next door. They would dress up in old curtains and one of them would be the queen and the other the princess and they'd have fancy tea parties with Juicy Juice and Oreos. Her mom would be the maid and ask if she could clear the "tea things" away. When she started school, she quickly learned she had a good singing voice. In the seventh grade musical, she'd played Oliver Twist and remembered how she had to pull her hair back and pin it up under her cap in order to play the part. She had the lead in eighth grade too. In high school, the competition got tougher, but she didn't give up when she didn't get the part she'd hoped for. This year she'd been cast for a major role in the winter musical. She fully intended to be involved with theatre in college and knew U of I had lots of opportunities. She'd find out if Beacon did. Then maybe she'd apply if her parents were okay with it.

When her dad came home, Katie told him all the same things she'd explained to her mom. He kept looking at her mom as if to ask is this a good idea, but she knew he'd go along.

Later, looking at the website more closely, Katie found Beacon had good theatre and psychology departments. She decided to apply for the regular admission deadline rather than for the early deadline because she wasn't sure enough about her choice. Her guidance counselor had explained that colleges that offered early action usually allowed you also to apply to other colleges. If you were admitted early you didn't have to enroll. Colleges that offered early decision would inform you if you were admitted or rejected. If you were admitted early decision you were required to enroll, unless the financial aid they offered was not sufficient.

Katie printed a copy of the application from the website and filled it out in pencil for practice. Some of her friends would think she was a little compulsive, but she liked things to be right.

A week later, when she'd finished drafting her essays, she asked Mr. Rossa to read them. He made a couple of minor suggestions, told her he thought they were fine, and that she should submit them. Mrs. Ritkowski was okay with them too. Finally, after she had proofread the pages at least five times, she clicked submit. The deed was done.

After her application was transmitted to Beacon's computer, Katie had to arrange for an interview with an alum living in her area. The web site explained that she should call Louise Torrell.

"Mom, I'm so busy, do you think you could call this Louise Torrell, the Beacon alum, and set up an interview for me," Katie asked, a little intimidated by the prospect.

"I'm not applying. You are. If you want to go all the way to Boston for college, you should be able to make a telephone call. You know your schedule better than I do."

"I just thought maybe you could help, but never mind, I'll call her when I get home this afternoon."

After her English class, Katie asked a classmate if she'd had any college interviews. She had. "Did you have to set them up?" Katie asked.

"I called the first interviewer and he and I met at that coffee shop on West Avenue. He was friendly and told me all about what he did when he was a student at Yale. Are you going to have an interview?"

"I'm applying to Beacon and I'm supposed

to call the interviewer."

"Just do it. Don't worry about it. Some colleges make you go to the campus for an interview, but others have volunteer alums in the area where you live."

When Katie came home from school, she found the interviewer's phone number. She wasn't sure if she wanted her to answer or not. After a few rings, a female voice said, "Hello."

"Hi, this is Katie Lorko. I've applied to Beacon and the website said I should call you to set up an interview."

"Oh. Hi, Katie. I'm Louise Torrell's mother. I'm babysitting for my grandson who's sick today. Louise will be home from work around six. Do you want her to call you or do you want to call her back?"

Katie had to think. "I'll call her back. What time would be good?"

"Around seven. "

After Katie and her parents ate spaghetti and salad for dinner, Katie said she had to call the college interviewer.

Katie tapped the phone number into her cell and waited while the phone rang, once, twice, three times. Oh no, she thought, she's not there.

"Hello," a man's voice said.

"Hi, this is Katie Lorko. Is Ms. Torrell there?"

"Hold on, I'll get her. Louise, it's for you," Katie heard him say.

"Hello," a woman's voice said.

"Ms. Torrell, this is Katie Lorko. I got your name from the Beacon website. I'm supposed to call you to set up an interview and..."

Ms. Torrell interrupted, "Katie, I'm glad to hear from you. I was told that you'd applied and I expected your call. I usually do interviews on Sunday evenings. I meet the candidates at the McDonald's on Main St. around seven in the evening. If that won't work for you, we can find another time."

"Next Sunday will be fine.

When Katie returned to the kitchen, her mom asked, "What happened? Were you able to set up an interview?"

"Yes, we're going to meet at McDonald's next Sunday at seven. I'll write it on the calendar."

On Sunday afternoon, Katie thought about what she should wear for the interview. She decided on her gray pants and cinnamon colored sweater. When she came downstairs, she asked her mom, "How do I look?"

"You look fine. Don't forget to ask Ms. Torrell what kinds of things she did at college and why she went there. I read a magazine article about admissions and it said that's a good thing to do."

"See you later," Katie said.

She drove to Main St. and parked in the McDonald's parking lot.

When Katie walked into the restaurant, she realized she wasn't sure how she would find Ms. Torrell. While she was standing near the trash containers, a woman came in, looked around, walked toward Katie and said, "Are you Katie Lorko?"

"Yes. Are you Ms. Torrell?"

"I am. I'm glad to meet you in person. Let's sit over there by the window." After they'd taken off their jackets, she asked if she could get Katie something, as she planned to buy a coffee for herself.

"I'm okay," Katie said.

"How about some tea, or a soda, or a smoothie? My treat."

"I guess a water would be good."

While she was gone, Katie pulled out a notepad and pen from her backpack.

After Ms. Torrell returned with their drinks, and pulled out her own notebook and pen from her pocketbook, she asked Katie to tell her why she'd decided to apply.

"My English teacher went to a conference where an Admissions person from Beacon spoke. He told me about it and said I should look at their website because he thought I'd like it there. They have a good theatre department and a good psychology program, I think. Is that true?" Katie asked.

Ms. Torrell agreed. "What else besides theatre do you like to do?"

"I write for the newspaper and play tennis, but I really like musical theater the best. I'm thinking of majoring in psychology. What did you major in?"

"I majored in biology and then taught high school for a few years. Now I'm working part time as a web designer. I guess that means the education I received gave me a good foundation for many things. Tell me a little bit about your family."

Katie explained how she was adopted and that she had no brothers or sisters.

"I have a friend who has just adopted a baby girl. Do you have any suggestions for her?"

"I think it's a good idea to explain why they adopted her as early as she can understand."

Katie asked what Ms. Torrell would do with the information she'd written down.

"I'll write a report, a page or two, of our meeting. I try to be positive unless the person seems like a sociopath. You don't. The Admissions Office says our reports give them a more filled in picture of the applicant."

As Katie drove back home, she wasn't sure what Ms. Torrell really thought of her.

CHAPTER TEN

Allie looked out the kitchen window and saw the January clouds. The thermometer said thirty-five degrees. Cold and gray, a perfect day for being inside in my red fleece vest, long sleeved gray jersey, and black corduroys, she thought. Sam I Am purred and arranged herself on the sofa. The aroma of green tea came from the cup given to her by the Singapore high school visitors. The room felt warm and cozy. She turned the radio on to a classical station. As she moved away, the music went static. "How annoying," Allie said to the cat. Before she could change the station, the noise stopped and the music came back.

After arranging the desk with the triaging guidelines, she turned on her computer and opened the first application. The telephone rang. Sam jumped off the couch. Allie hurried to pick up the phone.

"Hi," said one of her colleagues from the office who processed graduate applications before they were forwarded to the department. "I just got a call from the graduate English department. They want a spreadsheet of all applicants for the past five years with the names of their undergraduate colleges and whether they were admitted or not."

"Don't they have that information? Why do they need it from us?"

"Oh, you know. They think we have more time than they do. She knows we're busy, but her boss wants the information and she doesn't have anyone to pull it together. I told her I'd call you at home because you were reading freshman applications."

"Tell her we'll get the data. I need to get back to triaging or I'll never finish. See you tomorrow," Allie wrapped up the conversation, even though she would have preferred to keep talking.

Allie liked working at home in Newton. It was better than commuting thirty minutes among drivers intent on getting their way. On the other hand, there would be a lot of work to catch up on when she was back in the office tomorrow. Reading applications and making admissions decisions were the core elements of the work, but the time it took made her anxious about all the other aspects of her job.

Allie and other senior staff did triaging. They'd decide which applicants had little chance of being admitted either because they had grades, standardized test scores, or teacher evaluations that were less than stellar in their pool, or with a quick scan of their activities, no outstanding talent. A second group, who had good grades, good scores, good teacher evaluations, and some talent, would go on for a full second read. The second reads provided a fuller picture of the applicant and elaborated on whether the candidate had the match with Beacon's culture. Those who received a full second read would be acted by a committee of three people and either admitted, not admitted, or wait listed.

The group sent on for a full second read was the one from which the four hundred special admits would be selected without that read carried out, Allie thought. They would be admitted to test Marina's theory that being admitted by itself was enough to be successful even if they were not great matches.

In the morning, triaging always went faster. Later it would be a struggle to finish her quota of seventy applications. The workload might be more bearable if her boss seemed more appreciative, Allie thought. He doesn't spend enough time outside of his office. He didn't even notice when one of the staff assistants became pregnant. She could still hear his, "Did she have a baby?" when she passed the envelope to collect for a gift.

I can't keep thinking about other things. Keeping focused on the details in the applications was important, because the decision about whom to read more fully was often a result of the details. Allie remembered when the daughter of a well-known politician almost was triaged out and then denied admission because the staff person newly arrived from a far away state hadn't recognized the name. Someone else noticed. The applicant was triaged back in at least to receive a thorough read.

She quickly scanned the bio page. Had a parent or grandparent attended Beacon? Legacies received more personalized turndowns in order to keep good will.

Richard "Rick" Componella, 44 Tisbury Lane, Belleview, Nebraska, born May 13, 1994 in Omaha. Parents, Robert Componella and Lucy Hargis Camponella, farmer and farmer's wife. Two siblings, Carrie, age 15 and Cindy, age 12. Parents graduated from the University of Nebraska. No relatives were affiliated.

A quick scan of the teacher and guidance counselor ratings showed a top student. Transcript listed some AP courses with excellent grades. The summary cards filled out by references were also good.

She moved the applicant to the triaged in group. As she opened the next application, the telephone rang.

"Hi. It's Andy. How's it going?"

"Okay. I just read a good one. I kept waiting for the other shoe to drop, but nothing seems out of place and he's from Nebraska. What's up?"

"Max came into my office this morning.

He's been thinking about how to get the faculty more involved in our decision process and wanted to know if I thought it was a good idea to ask someone in the Architecture Department to read applications from those who think they'll major in architecture. Someone from that department called him to ask about reading. Maybe he thinks it will reduce our reading time."

"What did you tell him?"

"That giving the department input into who's admitted makes sense."

"That seems right. Well, I have to get back or I'll never finish. See you tomorrow."

By one o'clock she'd gone through more than half her quota. Allie knew the rules for triaging someone into the full read group, or "keeping them alive" in admissions lingo: always keep in mind that there are many more qualified applicants than spots for admitted students. Triaging too many into the full read group created unnecessary work for her colleagues. Was the process fair to the applicants? The bottom line was they could only admit as many as were needed to yield the number they had room to enroll because Beacon guaranteed housing for all freshmen.

She needed a break and decided to check her office voicemail. She heard a raspy voice say, "I have a question about admissions. My granddaughter, Courtney, is applying. Her guidance counselor told her Boston isn't a very safe city. I remember at the Omaha meeting you said the college area is pretty safe, that people are around at all hours of the night, and even on weekends. I'm worried about Courtney going so far away. Do you think Lincoln would be better for her?"

I'll get back to her when I'm in the office, Allie thought. I guess it makes sense to be concerned about safety when your child or grandchild is thinking of going so far from home. When Ann was applying to college, Bill and I had the same concerns. Ann hasn't texted me yet today. I wonder what she's doing.

Allie headed to the kitchen for lunch. Sam was right behind her. "Okay, Kitty, what will it be? Tuna? Salmon? Fancy Feast?" After she snapped the can lid open, Sam did her usual rubbing legs and purring routine. Allie watched the cat grab chunks of food and methodically chew and swallow with her chin tilted to the side. She thought about what she wanted for lunch. Looking into the refrigerator, she realized she'd forgotten to buy mushrooms for tonight's dinner. She called Bill's number, got his voicemail, and left a message for him to pick up the mushrooms and some milk on his way home.

She put a cup of water into the microwave for tea, opened the cabinet, and took out a black tea bag. She had to stay awake. After finishing her omelet and an apple, she thought about the lottery. Even though the experiment was supposed to be a secret, she had told Bill, a social psychologist at a different university, about it when Max had first discussed it with her. "It's a great chance to find out how important the match is," he'd said. "Doing research in a real life setting is a plus."

I can't keep worrying about the experiment. I need to get back to work. By early evening, one application was left. She forced herself to open it.

Kathryn Lorko. Date of birth, April 16, 1997. Parents, John and Carolyn Lorko. Place of birth, Chicago, Illinois. Favorite activity: acting. In response to the question, is there anything else not covered in your responses to other questions that you'd like us to know, Katie had written, "My parents adopted me right after I was born. I was told my birth mother gave me up for adoption because she wasn't ready for the responsibility of a baby. I'd always hoped to meet her, but a few years ago, I learned she'd died in an automobile accident."

Allie felt a rush of adrenalin. When did Katie say she was born? What's her last name? She went back to the bio section of the application: April 16. Could this be Paula's daughter? I can't believe what I'm seeing. I was with Paula that day, the day she had the baby. Can this be her? That would be too much of a coincidence. Calm down and think rationally. The adoptive family lived in Illinois. This family does. Is there a picture in the file? A picture of the cast of Brigadoon when Katie had played Fiona was attached. She didn't look exactly like Paula, but there was enough resemblance for Allie to believe that Katie could be Paula's daughter. Allie ran up the stairs to the closet where she kept a box of old letters and souvenirs. She found the envelope that she'd kept for many years. Inside the envelope Allie took out the piece of paper on which she'd long ago written, "Adoptive family name Lorko." It had to be her.

She'd never forget the day seventeen years earlier when Paula called, obviously upset, and said, "If I tell you something, you can't tell anyone."

"I promise," Allie replied.

" I just told my parents and Mom told me not to tell anyone so don't say anything if you see her."

"I won't. What's the matter?"

"I'm pregnant."

"Do you want to be?"

"No. I'm not ready to be a mother, but I don't want to have an abortion, even though I don't agree with most of that Catholic stuff anymore. Mom's cousin Jane in Illinois will help me. She's a nurse for an obstetrician. She lives in Northbrook. Mom called her and she said I could live with them. She's sure the doctor could arrange a private adoption."

"Do you want to get married?"

"Yes, but he's not the right person.

Over the following years, they had kept in

touch through email and at holidays, but about five years ago, when Paula, her husband, and son were returning to Massachusetts from skiing in Vermont, another driver crossed the median and Paula, her family, and the other driver were killed. At Paula's funeral, her widowed mother, Mrs. Kotski, spoke to Allie about her granddaughter who lived near Chicago. Now Allie asked herself again, why did Paula have to die? At high school parties Paula would play all the latest hits on the piano by ear. With her wavy auburn hair she'd looked like a young Katharine Hepburn. They'd gone to different colleges, but when Allie married Bill, Paula was her maid of honor.

After getting over the initial shock of finding Paula's daughter's application on her computer, and before she allowed herself any hope for this applicant, Allie took another look at the transcript: Mostly A's, top ten percent of her class, tests in the six fifty to seven fifty range, state ranked thespian, tennis talent, and newspaper reporter. Katie's definitely a cut above. She triaged the application in. Even though she'd had a long day, she started to do the full read right then. She wouldn't take a chance that Katie might get put in the group to be selected through the lottery. At least the application would go to the full committee.

Katie wrote in her essay that sometimes acting provided an opportunity to relax, to try out lives completely different. Since she planned to be a psychologist, she needed to develop an understanding of people's motivations, even those in plays. Kind of interesting. Maybe not the most compelling essay she'd ever read, but not bad.

Next Allie looked at the teachers' recommendations, the guidance counselor's report, and the interviewer's comments. All positive.

She shouldn't push for an applicant, but she couldn't help herself. We have to admit her, she thought. Even though she was special enough to be triaged in for a full read, the best applicants had to survive in a pool of stellar candidates when they came before the committee. She couldn't assume Katie would be admitted, though everything looked good. When committee decisions were made, some team member could be in a bad mood or not want to admit any more students from Chicago. Well, maybe it wasn't quite like that, but Allie knew she couldn't count on Katie's getting in. She hadn't won a national prize or invented a world-changing machine. No, Katie was a solid applicant with some distinction in her school and at state level theatre competitions. She was good, but so were many of the other applicants. Allie typed her initials, "Show A.L," onto the summary form on the screen. If the committee were inclined not to admit Katie, she would have a chance to argue for her. It was the best she could do.

CHAPTER ELEVEN

While Allie was at home triaging, Max was in the office. Peter Plank called to say that he and Alan had finished reading the old freshman applications.

"Alan and I divided up the files after going over a few of them to calibrate our guesses about who would do well in the introductory science courses the freshmen took to satisfy the core curriculum requirement. We spent the next week reading and rating their chances of getting A's and B's and then discussed our findings. Could we talk to you to see if we've guessed correctly? We could come by your office at two tomorrow."

"That's fine," Max said. "See you then." As annoyed as he sometimes felt about faculty interference, Max hoped that Peter and Alan would have some worthwhile suggestions for avoiding admitting "the wrong" freshmen. No one benefitted from that experience, not the students, not the faculty, not the admissions staff, not the families of the students, no one. He also knew that nothing they'd tried over the years had totally eliminated those who didn't pass the core, those who failed to graduate, or those who struggled through.

The next day, when Natalie told Max the professors were sitting in the reception area waiting to meet with him, he said to let Allie know, "Then have them come in."

"Tell me what you've found," he said as the two took seats facing his desk.

"We won't know what we've found until you tell us if we've correctly identified those who didn't do well," Peter said.

The telephone rang. Max told Peter and Alan he had to take the call, but they should stay right there. While he was waiting for Natalie to put the call through, he heard Peter say to Alan, "Is there anything about the applicant with the number id #007 that merited admission? I think it's a he. One of the recommendations had a "he" that hadn't been erased. He seems like a very mediocre applicant, especially compared with some of the others."

"I'm not sure, but I noticed the interviewer said something about seeing him at a soccer meet," Alan said. "Maybe he's a really good player. I know the athletic department has been trying to become more competitive in soccer."

"I'm not interested in athletics. I'm only interested in academics. These kids have to pass the core. No wonder we have more students doing poorly."

"I'm not sure that's true, Peter," Alan said. "I remember talking with someone from the Dean's Office who told me that even though more fail the first math or science quiz, by the end of the semester, the percentage getting grades lower than 'B' is no higher than it was five years ago."

"Do you believe everything they tell you? I'm not sure they don't adjust the numbers."

"I don't think they'd lie. Anyway, let's wait until Max gives us the results. Hi, Allie, how are you?" Alan added, as Allie came into the office.

Max nodded to her while holding the phone to his ear. "Here are the grade point averages at the end of the semester when they took their science courses," she said handing them sheets with applicants identified not by name but with codes from #001 through #100.

For the next few minutes, the professors transferred their yes/no guesses onto the grade sheets. Max ended his phone call.

"I'm a little surprised that Alan and I each correctly identified only a few students who got into serious academic trouble. Most of those we thought would do poorly finished the term with a C average at least. Some of those we thought would be stars weren't."

"I knew from previous analyses of freshman grades and high school data that identifying all those who would do poorly was almost impossible, but I half expected, maybe hoped, that you would find a way to pick them out," Max said. "That would have been a good thing for the admissions business, even if it meant changing how we do it. I'm disappointed you weren't able to do better."

Peter said he knew other studies of the relationship between high school records and performance of undergraduates had been done, "Could we see the data?" Allie left to get the reports.

Before she rejoined the group, Peter told Max that his neighbor's son would be applying and that he would make an excellent student. Max wrote himself a note to that effect. "Thanks. I'll keep an eye out for his application. Did you find the reports?" he asked Allie.

"Here they are. If you want anything copied, I'll do it," she said as she handed out reports of the two most recent studies involving freshman grades and high school records to Peter and Alan.

"Why don't you take the reports over to the table by the window and look through them," Max said. "I have some messages to respond to. Allie can answer any questions you have."

As Peter and Alan read through the reports, Max tried to figure out how to give a diplomatic email response to a high school guidance counselor from Rhode Island who wanted to spend a few months as a volunteer in the Admissions Office. She hoped to be useful by answering email, talking to visitors, sitting in on staff meetings, reading applications, and participating in decision making in order to learn the business from the "other side." The Admissions Office would get an extra staff person at no cost she wrote. In some ways the offer was tempting, but Max could hear what Priscilla would say— "Somebody is going to have to train her before she talks to or meets with anyone and that person will be me and I just don't have any extra time. It isn't worth it"—and Max knew Priscilla would be right. Whenever someone outside the office wanted to read applications or travel to meet high school students, they were usually not prepared for the intensity and pace of the work. Most people enjoyed travel and reading for pleasure, but doing it for work was different. Traveling to eight different cities in two weeks was more like a forced march. He emailed the guidance counselor that he appreciated her interest, but at this time they were unable to accommodate any extra personnel. He hoped she would understand. If she were in the Boston area, he would be happy to talk with her.

Just as he was finishing with the email, he heard Alan say to Peter, "It almost seems like Admissions could put the names of everyone with good grades and good scores into a hat and pick them that way."

"Don't say that," Peter said. "Can you imagine the publicity if word got out? On the other hand, the hat might do as well as some of these Admissions staff."

Max felt his stomach tighten. If Peter found out about the lottery, he'd have a lot of explaining to do. Was the experiment really worth it? Even though some faculty might be intrigued by the idea, others, like Peter, might be angry. What if the secret got out?

"Max, Alan and I have a question. It seems from these studies you've done that not only is it difficult to know who won't do well in the core, it's also hard to tell who will become a real academic star by graduation. You say unless students have high scores and grades there's virtually no chance they'll receive top grades, but of that group, it's been hard to predict who will be special in other ways. Is there anything we could measure that would increase that prediction? What if we had them do some sort of creative project as part of the admissions process?"

"We're nervous about giving what they do on their own outside of school or not in organized activities too much weight. There's no way to know how much help they've received."

"That's true, I guess, but don't we have to depend on the integrity of the applicants?" Alan asked.

"Yes, but President Reagan was on the mark when he said trust but verify. Obviously, we can't check every fact for every applicant, but some of us have had experience with our own kids when we've "helped" more than we should have. I understand what you're after here; I'm just nervous that we won't be evaluating the applicant's, but rather the parent's, the teacher's, or some other paid counselor's ability. I don't want to put down any new ideas you have, though. If you can come up with something we could add to the application process that we could do and both of you would be willing to evaluate in a year or two, we could give it a try."

"I don't know," Allie said, "if you read the story in this week's *Spotlight* about Paul L'Arcane, the assistant professor in computer science?"

The three shook their heads no, though Peter added, "Not more hype about the wonder kid! Enough already!"

"I remember meeting him when he was a senior in high school," Allie continued. "He has a great personality, but I never would have guessed what a star he would become. I can't imagine what set him apart. I hope you can find some predictors of that kind of special success, but I'm not optimistic."

"We faculty have had more experience with superstars. We'll think about what might be added to the application to identify them," Peter said.

"Thanks for your help," Max said as they got up to leave. "In some ways it's good to know we haven't been missing something obvious about who might excel."

"That's over for now," he said to Allie

after Peter and Alan were gone. "Why don't they just do their jobs and let us do ours? I guess we have to accept the fact that in a university like this, the faculty think they're in charge."

"Even though they weren't able to come up with a better algorithm for admitting students who would get A's and B's in the science core, the fact that we know they're concerned about mediocre students might result in our being more cautious when we admit those whose scores or grades are a little less strong," Allie said. "On the other hand, now that they understand it's not that easy to completely avoid students who will have trouble, maybe they'll find a better way to teach less well-prepared students, a way that will insure a greater degree of success for all. It could have a positive result, or maybe I have to think that way to justify the amount of time it's taken to get everything together for their experiment."

"I'm not certain they've learned anything from the reading they did, but if they can come up with something realistic to identify superstars, we could try it for a year or two and see how much information we gain and then decide whether or not to continue," Max said. "I need to get back to answering my emails."

After Allie left, he closed the door and clicked his computer to life. The Dow Jones had lost a hundred and thirty points that day.

CHAPTER TWELVE

"Anything new with you?" Allie asked Maggie as they walked to the parking garage.

"We haven't actually talked for awhile. Do you have time now?"

"Sure," Allie said as they kept walking.

"Last fall, I was the only one in the office after five. Nice and quiet. No phones ringing. My report for the Neighborhood Alliance was written. I was standing by the printer, when I heard a knock. The doors were locked and I expected it to be someone looking for Andy or Natalie. Instead it was Jack Bradmore, a faculty member from the Architecture Department, who said he had an appointment with Max at five thirty. I noticed blue eyes that were almost turquoise."

"I remember meeting him once," Allie said. "He's nice looking with sandy hair, about six feet tall?"

"Yes. I introduced myself, told him Max must have forgotten because he'd left, and asked if I could help. He said Max was going to discuss the possibility of his reviewing applications from students who want to major in architecture and that we could use help evaluating drawings or other work. He said he'd come back another time. I told him I knew what Max wanted to talk to him about, that I was part of an Admissions group trying to figure out how faculty from departments applicants say they intend to major in can participate in the process. I added that if he was interested in helping, we would screen out any applicants with low grades and test scores and give him only those with a chance of being admitted."

"Did you tell him most of the reading could be done during the semester break?"

"Yes. He said he was always here working on his research anyway. I told him it probably wouldn't take more than about twenty minutes to read the application to decide if the applicant seemed like a good prospect. He could enter his comments online. One of the staff would do a regular read of those he liked. I noticed he wasn't wearing a wedding ring."

"What happened? It's not too cold. Let's sit down here on this bench."

"Okay. As Jack was leaving, he said he needed to eat before going to a meeting. He asked if I was interested in continuing our conversation over some food."

"You went?"

"I told him I had a conservation meeting later in Charlestown where I lived, but I needed to eat, too. While we ate, I asked him how long he'd been at Beacon. Two years. I told him I was in my third year, that I enjoyed my job, but like everyone else, felt I didn't have as much time as I'd like for other things. He said he didn't know how people with kids managed. I was glad to hear he didn't have kids.

"Where does he live?"

"He said about six blocks from here. He asked me about living in Charlestown. I told him the same thing I tell everyone, that I love living there even though it's a little more expensive than I expected. We sat upstairs in the cafeteria. We talked about all sorts of things."

"Have you seen him since?"

"He was interested in touring Charlestown so we set a time for the following Sunday. A few days later, I was walking down the hallway near our office toward the front lobby, when I saw him ahead of me with a beautifully dressed woman. They were talking and not paying attention to anything else. The woman was holding his arm. Before I saw them, I'd been thinking about the walk we'd planned, maybe even counting too much on the possibilities. Anyway, without exactly knowing why, I turned around and walked the other way, all the while wondering how good a friend the woman was. I knew I couldn't compete with someone who looked like that."

"I know what you mean. What happened?"

"The Sunday morning we were supposed

to meet in Charlestown to look at the sights, the phone rang. It was Jack. He said something had come up, that he wouldn't be able to meet me. We rescheduled for two weeks later."

"You must have been disappointed."

"I was. I wished he'd told me why he couldn't make it. I had visions of him with that woman. I tried not to think about it and didn't run into him during the two weeks. My ex-boyfriend, the one who lives in New York, called one day and asked if I wanted to come to the city for a weekend. We're still friends and I thought about going. But I didn't really feel like it, and besides, work is busy."

"Two weeks must have seemed a long time."

"Finally, that Sunday came and it was a nice day. Sunny and not too cold. I wondered if he'd show up or if something else would interfere. He'd said he'd come to my place around eleven. By ten forty-five, I'd straightened up the living room, taken my jacket from the closet, watered the plants, and tried to read *The Sunday Globe*. At eleven, the phone rang. Not again I thought. I knew I'd been too hopeful about the day's possibilities. When I answered, it was my friend Pat who wanted to know if I could have lunch. I told her I'd love to, but that I was expecting someone who wanted to see Charlestown. The doorbell rang. It was Jack."

"What a relief."

"He said he hadn't had breakfast or lunch, and wondered if I'd mind getting something to eat before we started the tour. We went to The Backyard, that restaurant on the water."

"I love that place," Allie said.

"We had a table with a view of the ferry dock and ordered Bloody Mary's, eggs Benedict, and coffee. After we'd finished eating, we sat for awhile then noticed a line waiting for tables so we left."

"Did you go to the Bunker Hill Monument?"

"Of course; before that, we saw Old Ironsides and some of the historic homes. After climbing all the Monument stairs up and down, we were ready for a break. We started walking toward the Warren Tavern when Jack's phone rang. He said he was sorry, but he had to leave. I'd have to give him a rain check. We walked back to my condo where his car was parked. He said he enjoyed lunch and the tour, that he'd like to see more, and would give me a call as soon as he could free up some time. He shook my hand for quite awhile. I told him I'd had a good time."

"So what happened? Have you heard from him?"

"At staff meeting in November when Priscilla told everyone that applications would be ready for reading by that Friday and we'd better plan on working the weekend, I thought there goes my social life. On Thursday, when I was packing up at the end of the day, the phone rang. It was Jack asking if I had time for a drink. We met in the front lobby and walked to the Miracle of Science, where we sat at the bar and ordered a couple of Stellas."

"And?

"I asked him if he went there often. He said he did. It's kind of his neighborhood place. His condo is only a few blocks away. We talked about architecture. He's just started working with a grad student who has some interesting ideas about conservation design. He said he wished he'd been an architect in the era of cheap energy and could design buildings with only beauty in mind. But he also likes the challenge of melding environmental concerns with the design."

"Did you tell him more about your conservation group?"

"I did: that our Charlestown group tries to strategize new ways to go green, that we don't want to make life harder, but to make conserving more natural. When we walked back toward the parking garage, he asked if I'd like to attend a lecture sponsored by his department the following Tuesday. The speaker was coming from Yale and was on the cutting edge of research that deals with integrating environmental concern with good design. I said I'd go."

"Did you?" Allie asked.

"Yes, but when I walked into the lecture room looking for Jack, I saw him standing next to the same woman I'd seen him with in the hall a few weeks before. I didn't know whether to stay or leave, but before I could decide, he hurried over with the woman following. He introduced me to Sofia Solatte who teaches architecture at MIT. The Department Chair asked everyone to be seated so the talk could begin. The three of us sat on the left side of the room. I noticed Peter Plank take a seat on the other side."

"Peter Plank? He's interested in Architecture?"

"Jack gave Peter a little wave. The talk was good enough that I was able to listen and not spend the entire time wondering about Jack's relationship to Sofia or to Peter. After everyone asked questions, we were invited to a wine and cheese reception in the lounge. I got up planning to leave, but Jack refused to hear my excuses, took my arm, walked me toward the reception area, with Sofia following. He got wine for all of us. I felt like draining my glass in one gulp, but managed to hold onto it for at least five minutes. Jack noticed my glass was empty and went to get another."

"Did you find out how Jack knows Sofia?"

"Sofia asked me how I knew Jack. I told her he was helping Admissions read applications from students who think they might major in architecture. I asked her how she knew him. Before she could answer, Jack came back with my wine and Peter. Jack introduced everyone. Peter Plank is his cousin. Oh, look at the time. I need to get going. I'll tell you the rest, but let's start walking toward the garage."

"Funny. I never think people like Peter have cousins. Don't you find him kind of an odd guy? Sometimes he doesn't seem to notice me when I pass him in the hall."

"I know what you mean. Peter launched into the points on which he agreed and disagreed with the speaker. Something he said got Sofia's interest. While the two of them were going on about it, Jack asked me if I found the talk relevant to my conservation work. I told him I did and that I didn't know he was Peter's cousin. He said Peter was his mother's cousin and they hadn't known each other well, but when he applied for the job, she sent Peter an email, just in case he had any pull. Then he said, 'Hey, Peter, I was just telling Maggie, your influence is why I got the job.' He also said he and Peter enjoy arguing with each other, or sometimes just talking."

"Did you ever find out how Jack knows Sofia?"

"Just when I began to feel like a fifth wheel and was thinking about how to make my exit, Sofia started to wave at someone across the room. This tall, dark-haired, very handsome guy came over. Sofia introduced him. His name is Antonio Testaverde and get this, he's her fiancé."

"Interesting."

"Jack said Antonio is how he knows Sofia. Antonio was Jack's college roommate.

They're both handsome, though very different looking. We all kept talking, drinking wine, and eating cheese and crackers, until Peter looked at his watch and said he had to run to get the train. I didn't want to leave, but felt I should. Before I could say anything, Antonio asked if we wanted to get something to eat at this new place he'd heard about that was just a few minutes away. I said I had some work to do, but the three of them insisted I go. At dinner they got to talking about how if Admissions could simplify the process, I'd have a lot more free time. I said I wished we could do it."

"That must have been scary having that topic come up. Do you think you'll see more of Jack?"

"We already have plans," Maggie said as they reached Allie's car.

"How do you feel about the lottery?" Allie asked. "Personally, I'm okay with it, but every now and then I get nervous thinking about all the things that could go wrong. What if some faculty member finds out and thinks we're lowering standards even if we're not, or if some reporter decides to make a name for himself by doing an exposé of admissions staff being lazy? There are all kinds of things I can imagine."

"You told me that Bill said it was a good opportunity and that we should do it," Maggie said. "It makes me a little anxious, but I like the idea of having more free time."

"I guess it'll be okay. There's my car."

"Wait. I need to tell you something." Maggie said. "I accidentally mentioned the experiment to Jack. The two of us had a few more drinks and were having a good time and I said we were trying to find a way to get our applications read without increasing the number of staff so we were doing this experiment to find out if the match was as important as we all think. We were admitting some applicants with good grades and scores by lottery without full reads. I realized what I'd said and made him swear not to tell anyone. He said he wouldn't."

"Max never should have agreed to carry out a secret project like this. He had to know it's impossible for so many people to keep a secret. You told Jack, I told Bill. I'm sure everybody told someone. You don't think Jack would say anything to Peter, do you?"

"I think he knows we need to keep this quiet."

Allie hoped that was true. She got into her car worried that too many people outside of the office knew about the experiment. What if one of them told someone who told someone else? What if a reporter found out? She never should have supported Max's crazy idea.

CHAPTER THIRTEEN

On a cold and sunny February day, Allie walked in the door earlier than usual. She heard voices coming from several internal offices. People were already in. Today, and for the next couple of weeks, they would meet in committees of three to admit next fall's freshman class. Regular action was a bigger version of the early action admissions process they'd carried out in December. Then, they could avoid making final decisions on many applicants by deferring them to this regular action cycle. Now, the only escape hatch they would have would be the waitlist. If they couldn't justify an admission and didn't want to reject an applicant, they could put the person on the waitlist, the purgatory of admissions. It was exciting to take part in the process but in addition to the sense of something special in the air, Allie felt a little anxious about working closely with colleagues who for most of the year were independent agents.

She checked her email, responding to those needing immediate answers. With mug in hand, she left for the committee room. Several large tables were piled high with summary sheets representing those applicants who had been triaged in for full reads. Each summary sheet had two ratings for each applicant: one representing the applicant's academic potential as shown by grades and standardized test scores, and another rating for achievement in non-classroom activities including leadership, sports, music, dance, really whatever. This morning they would act on those with pairs of top ratings. Andy and Maggie were already eating bagels and drinking coffee.

"Can you believe it's that time again?" Andy asked.

"No. It always comes so fast. It seems like we'll be reading forever. Then it's done and we're here," Allie said as she poured herself hot water from the water dispenser and then took an English breakfast tea bag from the tin. She sat by one of the large windows that overlooked the grassy courtyard, appreciating the last few moments before she'd need to join in and be part of a group where intensity and focus would be paramount.

More staff came into the room, some quietly, others exhibiting more enthusiasm than she felt. She'd been through many committee meetings, and even though she liked the work, the process was exhausting. Her mind would be numb by the end of the day.

Max said, "Let's get started. This morning

we'll divide up the top group." He began to read the names of those who would be working together. As their names were mentioned, Allie saw people move around to form their committees. Some groups preferred working near a window, others as far away as they could get from everyone else. The distance from one end of the room to the other was no more than thirty feet and six groups of three had to find space within the area to make their decisions. The Office had a tradition that all committees met in the same room at the same time, a room temporarily set up with extra tables on which the summary cards were arranged in piles depending on their academic and personal ratings that reflected their non-classroom involvement. People learned the need to work quietly in order not to disturb others. Even so, during the day the noise level would rise and fall. If some voices got especially loud, other staff would look over and try to figure out what was going on. Max called Allie's name listed with two others. She sat down in the center chair with the others on either side. They began to read and discuss the first case.

By noon, all the committees were ready to quit for lunch. "Is the office paying?" Andy asked.

"No, you're on your own today," Natalie said and looked around the room. Most people would go to check their email and voicemail and forage for food either in the lunch bags they'd brought with them or at one of the nearby cafeterias.

During the lunch break, Max went back to his office and shut the door. He congratulated himself on how well the morning had gone. He had been a committee of one, reading through the cases of applicants who were considered unlikely admits even though they'd initially been triaged in for a full second read. Relative to others in the triaged in pool, their ratings were at the bottom of that group: their scores and grades were very good, but not the best, and their activities made them interesting, but not as interesting as others; in general their ratings were lower.

When the telephone rang, he looked at the caller ID, saw it was Peter Plank, and considered letting the call go to voice mail. He knew that after the call he would not feel as good about the day, but he picked up the phone anyway. "Hi, Peter."

"Sorry to bother you, but Alan and I want to talk before you make admissions decisions."

"We've already started," trying to keep the irritation from his voice. "It would be difficult to change what we're doing,"

"We can come this afternoon."

"If you think it's something I need to hear. When?"

"Three o'clock?"

"All right, see you then." He added Peter's name to his calendar. Peter could have called earlier, Max thought, especially if he had information important to the admissions process. Max knew that most of the faculty did not concern themselves with the admissions business for undergraduates. A few, however, more than made up for them. It wasn't worth alienating those like Peter, who not only wielded power within the university, but also were aggressive in promoting their views.

Before one thirty, most of the staff had drifted back to the committee room. Max came in and saw Andy clearing the tables of used paper cups, napkins, crackers, donuts, cookies, and crumpled post its. He announced the new committees and said they could start going through the cases that fell into the group with the second best pair of ratings since they'd finished the top ratings group that morning. "I have to leave around three to meet with Peter Plank and Alan Overton. They want to communicate something they think we should know before we make any more decisions."

Maggie groaned more loudly than the rest, but they all kind of groaned. "What do they expect? That we can just change what we're doing?" Maggie complained.

"We're not going to make any changes that slow us down," Max said, while at the same time wondering what he could say to Peter to convince him to back off. "Let's get started. We'll stop around four."

Around three o'clock, Natalie came in and said to Max, "Peter Plank and Alan Overton are waiting in your office."

"Hi, Peter, Alan. What information do you have for me?" Max said as he sat down behind his desk. "You know we probably won't be able to make any significant changes now that we've started making decisions."

"We just want to talk. If you had to teach some of these freshmen…" Peter started to say.

Alan quickly interrupted, "Let's get right to it. We don't want to take any more of your time than we need to. Even though our reading experiment wasn't conclusive, we think you should have threshold SAT scores for admits."

"What about those who submit a TOEFL?" Max asked.

"What is a Tofu?" Alan inquired.

"Test of English as a Foreign Language," Max answered.

"I don't know." Peter said. "Why does it matter?"

"Well sometimes applicants whose native language isn't English use the TOEFL option, but maybe they also take the SAT, so all the scores come in, but only the TOEFL counts in computing the rating of their scores."

"You mean we admit students who can't really speak English? How can they understand the textbooks if they can't understand English?" Peter complained.

"Maybe we should take another look at those cases we read and see how the TOEFL figured in," Alan offered.

"If you can do it right away, there's a

chance we could use the information, otherwise it'll have to wait until next year," Max responded.

"Even though I don't think I approve of this TOEFL option," Peter said as they were leaving, "we'll do it right away and get back to you."

Max was about to head back to the committee room when the telephone rang.

"Hi, Marina," Max said as he leaned against the desk. "What's up?"

"How's the selection going? Have you picked the four hundred random admits yet?"

"We put the names of the all those the triagers identified to be read into a hat, pulled four hundred, and voila, we have the special admits."

"I can't believe we're really doing this. This is so great and especially that Skinner is okay with it."

"He knew we were going to do it and he hasn't changed his mind. We can talk more later, but I have to get back to committee now. I'll call you when we're done." The thought crossed his mind that maybe he shouldn't have been so eager to engage in this particular psychology experiment. He still retained his usual self-confidence, but was a little concerned about Marina's involvement and the importance to her of her own agenda.

Walking into the committee room, the noise level assaulted him. He couldn't believe any work was being done. Someone was reading an essay an applicant had written that had the rest of the room laughing. "People, people, we need to get through as many as we can. Let's get back to work," he shouted above the roar. The committees turned back to their own cases with some whispered remarks.

"Our group is looking at a top gymnast who can't take the tests until after the score deadline date. Her grades are perfect and she's very accomplished. Do we really need to have the scores from ETS? "

"Yes, we have to have the scores sent from the Educational Testing Service or from ACT," Priscilla said. "Don't you remember the applicant who forged her credentials including the transcript? We'd decided to admit her, but someone said that we needed to find her test scores. I took the case to the records room. Back then, when we had paper files, sometimes a copy of scores was included even though the scores are added to the database directly from the testing service website. The folder had no paper copy of scores. I called ETS and spoke to someone who couldn't find any record for the applicant. I called the high school, but the guidance counselor didn't know her, and couldn't find her listed among registered seniors. I called the alum who had done the interview. He distinctly remembered her. The bottom line is, if we hadn't had a requirement that all scores be sent directly from the testing company electronically, that applicant with the forged credentials would have been admitted."

While Priscilla was talking, Max felt increasingly anxious about the random admits. What would happen if someone found out what they'd done, or even worse, before they knew if the students' freshman grades would be okay? They wouldn't have a clue about how they would do at least until January of next year. However because he wanted to do this experiment and wanted it to work, he decided he'd have to put his nervous thoughts into a separate box in his mind and lock that box until the results were in. His wife had taught him that trick and he was always amazed at how well it worked. He turned the key in his mind lock box and went back to evaluating the applicants in the least competitive group until it was time to quit.

Half the people in the room escaped as soon as they could and the other half stayed to figure out how many they'd admitted. Before he left, Max looked around and saw James and Priscilla looking at the numbers of admits, not admits, and wait listed. Natalie was carrying a trash bag around and throwing in the half eaten food, used post its, paper cups, bottles, Hershey kiss wrappers, and decaying fruit. Andy was looking at a menu, and then asked Natalie, "Do you remember that kid who showed up in the office last year right after the admission notices went out? He hadn't been admitted and wanted to see if he could get the decision changed. He asked for me because we'd talked on the phone once.

He drove from New Jersey during the night to get here to plead his case. He was so intense I was worried, but had to tell him the decision was final. I asked about the other colleges where he'd applied, trying to get him to think more positively, and was able to reassure myself that he was emotionally stable enough to drive home."

"I do remember. You called his guidance counselor and told her you were worried."

"She told me she'd speak to him when he came back to school. She did and called back to say no serious problem. I guess he'd just taken to heart those newspaper stories about making personal contact with an admissions person as a way of increasing your chances of being admitted."

Max heard the phone ring as he walked into his office. Oh no, he thought as he looked at the caller ID. "Max Danker, here."

"Hi, Max. It's Chuck Skinner. I had a call this morning from *The Boston Globe*. Before I return it and ask them to call you if it's about admissions, I thought I'd better check. You don't think they know we're admitting some applicants by lottery?"

"I doubt it," he said as he crossed his fingers behind his back, while wondering, or do they? "The few people here who know wouldn't talk," he said while thinking, they wouldn't would they?

"If they ask me anything about it, we may need to change what we're doing. I don't want a story that makes us look less selective, you know what I mean?"

"I do know what you mean. I hope that's not why they called. I think they'll want to know the usual stuff like how many applicants, the number we plan to take, and so on. We've picked the four hundred we plan to admit randomly. Only Marina and a few of my top staff, who've helped with the selection, know. I think it'll be okay," Max offered while noticing a funny feeling in the pit of his stomach.

"All right," Chuck said. "I'll call *The Globe* back."

Next Max listened to a message from the Dean of Financial Aid who said her office needed the names of admits as soon as possible so the staff could evaluate their financial need.

Natalie came into his office and said there was a reporter from *The Globe* on the line. "I'll take the call," Max said.

The person on the other end of the line identified himself and then said, "I was talking to someone connected with the college who told me that Admissions might be doing something different this year. Can you speak to that?"

An electric tingle went up Max's spine. "One thing we're doing differently is related to financial aid, specifically that loans are being replaced by grants for families reporting income less than $90,000."

"I know about the financial aid, but someone told me there's something different about how you're making decisions. Are you using the same criteria to admit students this year as you have in the past?"

Max cleared his throat, and then said, "Who told you that?" Who could have called the *Globe*, Max wondered? I can't believe anyone from my staff would do that. Maybe he's heard something else. I can't jump to conclusions that he knows about the experiment.

"I'm not at liberty to give you that information. It's someone familiar with your office."

"As you probably know, not all admits are exactly the same, but everyone has to have something special. We don't count the number of extracurricular activities an applicant has. We focus on the passion for a particular activity. Maybe that's what you've heard?"

The reporter thought it was something different. He would check and call back.

Max could hear the reporter typing before hanging up. His own hands were sweaty. Who could have called the reporter? Should he change his mind about the experiment? Was it worth a year of tension? He needed to get all this back into his compartmentalized mind box—he wanted to find out if taking the extra time to make decisions the traditional way resulted in better students.

Later that week, the committees were reviewing the overwhelming number of application summaries piled in the middle of the table grid where the stacks were the highest. Around two, Allie told Max she needed to call someone in the president's office who wanted information about a major donor's child who might be an applicant.

A few minutes later, Max, who was sitting near Priscilla's group overheard her say, "Allie says she wants to be told when this case comes to committee." He saw Priscilla look around. "Allie's not here, but let's make the decision to admit, not admit, or waitlist anyway. I think we should do what we want and ask her opinion later. I'm not wowed by this girl."

The younger team members appeared surprised that she'd go ahead since Allie had asked specifically to be told when the case came up for review. When they finished reading the summary, one of the younger team members said, "I don't know. She doesn't look that special to me. She's an actress and a good tennis player and writes food reviews for the paper, but where's her leadership?"

"It says here that she started a program to help seventh grade girls with personal problems," the other team member said. "That shows leadership, I think. She's also gone to state level in the high school theatre competition."

"She looks kind of ordinary to me," the first team member repeated.

Priscilla looked ready to enter the 'N' for not admit, but instead said, "She's adopted and her parents aren't college graduates. I think we should take her. What do you think?" The other team members enthusiastically agreed. Max recalled that Priscilla herself had been adopted.

When Allie returned, Priscilla called over to say they had taken Katie Lorko. "You asked to be told when she came up."

"She seemed interesting to me. I knew her mother a long time ago," Allie said wondering whether she'd have to say anything else.

"Okay."

"Thanks." Relief washed over her. Maybe she could meet Katie if she came to visit during campus preview weekend.

CHAPTER FOURTEEN

Katie couldn't believe she'd been accepted at Beacon. Her parents could, and they were a little unnerved to think of her moving so far away. After the initial moods of surprise and exhilaration stabilized for all of them, she and her mother carefully read the information in the acceptance email, especially the invitation to visit for a few days in April, with or without parents.

"I'm supposed to reply and let them know if I plan to come. Do you think I should go? Can we afford it? Will you be able to come too?" she excitedly asked her mom.

"I think we should all go. We can get the time off. Where did they say you could stay? How about us?"

"I can stay with a student in a dorm and you have to stay in a hotel. Maybe we can visit the town where my birth mother grew up."

"There won't be enough time, but if you decide to enroll, we can visit then. If you don't enroll, we can still make a trip to see the town, if you want."

Several weeks later, Katie and her parents flew out of Chicago's O'Hare on a Thursday morning and arrived at Logan Airport two and a half hours later.

The Lorkos had visited Boston three years before, so they knew it was a small city compared with Chicago. The campus preview information gave them details about what to expect after they arrived at the airport. Students would greet them and help them locate the shuttle buses to the university. They waited in the baggage claim area for what seemed a long time to reclaim Katie's mom's bag, though it probably was only ten minutes or so. "If you hadn't checked your bag, we could be out of here," Katie complained.

Carolyn Lorko stood next to parents with a teenager. She asked her counterpart mom if they were in Boston to visit Beacon. The other family was not there for a university visit but had grandparents in the area. "Mom, not everyone who's here is visiting Beacon," Katie hissed. When her mom's luggage finally appeared, they turned themselves around toward the exit doors. They noticed a young woman holding a large sign, lettered "BEACON UNIVERSITY." Her dad went over and explained they were here for preview weekend. The tall brunette with perfect white teeth introduced herself, shook Katie's hand, told them to go to the bus stop area outside, and look for another student who would show them where they could get the shuttle bus.

So far so good Katie thought. The plane

flight was uneventful—the best kind—their luggage was in their possession, and they'd found a friendly and helpful student. When they walked through the exit doors, a blast of frigid air came as a surprise because the day was so sunny. After the wind off the lake in Chicago, Katie was not daunted, just a little cold.

"Brrr, I was hoping we'd get warmer weather," Katie's mom said as she lifted the collar of her black down jacket up around her neck.

"At least we're used to the cold," her dad said as he zipped up his blue parka with the Thinsulate lining. "Imagine what it's like if you're from California."

"I think if I lived in California, I'd stay there," Katie added as they herded their suitcases toward the young man with the Beacon sign standing in the middle island waving at them.

"Hi. You're here for the preview weekend?" As they all shook hands and introduced themselves, he asked, "Where are you from?"

"We're from Chicago," Katie's mom said. "Is this where we wait for the shuttle bus?"

"Yes, this is the place," he confirmed, just as he noticed another family heading toward him. He excused himself.

"Are you warm enough?" her mom asked looking at Katie.

"I'm fine," she replied looking toward the other family, also a mother, father, and daughter. The mother was wearing a long leather coat and high heeled boots, the father wore a black raincoat, and the daughter had on a dark gray wool coat, beautiful black leather boots, and a cream colored scarf tied in an elegant knot around her neck. With her long, straight, almost white blonde hair, Katie thought she looked like some modern fairy princess. She was sorry she'd followed her mother's advice to wear her short blue parka similar to her father's. The Beacon student seemed really interested in that girl with the blonde hair. They were talking non-stop. Maybe it was a big mistake to have come, Katie thought. Maybe U of I is more my kind of place.

Just then, the other family came over to the Lorkos. The daughter introduced herself and her parents, and extended her hand to shake Katie's. While everyone was shaking hands and repeating names so everyone would know everyone else, the blonde, whose name was Marybeth, kept talking. "I was so amazed to be accepted, weren't you? I can't believe I'm really here, how about you?"

Just then a large bus with "Yankee" lettered on its side drove up. The Beacon student motioned for them to get on. "Have a great time. If you come to the Beta house look for me. I'll introduce you around," he said, while looking at both Marybeth and Katie.

The bus was crowded, but there were seats for the Lorkos and the other family toward the back.

Katie overheard some mother with a southern accent complaining to her son about the name "Yankee" on the side of the bus. "You'd think they'd use a different bus service. Don't they know they'll have people from the south on board?" Katie thought she must have misheard. How could anyone complain about the name of a company being Yankee when they were in New England?

The bus made another stop at the international terminal where new arrivals speaking a foreign language that sounded like Greek and probably was, got on, taking the remaining single seats scattered throughout. At that point, a young woman seated in the front row stood up. With the aid of a microphone attached to her collar, she introduced herself, said she was a junior, and happy to meet them all. She gave a mini tour as the bus left the airport area. She said everyone would be dropped off near the student center where both students and parents needed to register for the preview weekend. Students would meet their overnight hosts and parents would receive directions to their hotels.

In addition she said there were a few sessions designed for both parents and their children, with the main one tomorrow's opening welcome at ten o'clock. Although most people would arrive today, the official opening was always scheduled for the next day to allow those travelers arriving later this evening to attend. Parents asked more questions about food and safety. Soon passengers were talking together. Only a few of the admitted students were without parents. Her mom was trying to engage one of them in conversation, Katie noticed. Once on campus, the bus pulled into a designated parking spot across the quadrangle from the student center. The student guide stood up and said, "Follow me."

Katie and her parents became part of the pack rolling or carrying their luggage toward the student center. Katie overheard her mom talking to another mother whose son was jogging ahead. The mother and son were from Ann Arbor. The woman's husband, a history professor at the University of Michigan, was involved with a dissertation defense scheduled long ago and would not arrive in Boston until the next day. When Katie's mom asked where they were staying, the other mother said that since her husband had done his graduate work at Beacon, they still had friends in the area, and would be staying with them.

Katie walked with her father, who kept commenting on how nice the campus looked and how many buildings there seemed to be. I'm not sure this is the right place for me, Katie thought, what if I don't meet anyone I like? Everyone else's parents look like they've been to college. I wish I hadn't come. Maybe we can go home early. Just then a cute guy walked over and asked if he could carry her bag. He insisted, so she gave it to him. He told her he was a biology major from Corpus Christi.

By the time they reached the student center, left their bags, and followed the group to the reception area, Katie said to her parents, "I'm glad we came. Are you?"

Her mom agreed. They joined the registration line. Parents were smiling and talking to other parents or to their child, or children, as younger brothers and sisters were part of some family groups. Often the younger ones were walking around the room, peering out the windows, wandering back to their families, and looking as if they knew they were in a place of great importance, even if they didn't quite know why.

Katie reached the front of the line, where the reception worker, Allie Lobelle, according to her nametag, who was busy looking at her list, said, "Hi. Last name?"

"Lorko. Katie."

"Oh. Thank you." Allie looked up at Katie, and didn't say anything right away. "Let's see. You have two parents with you?"

"Yes, we're all here."

"I'm so glad to meet you," Allie said smiling at Katie. "You'll find your hostess in the food lounge. Here's the final program with the events everyone is expected to attend listed on the first page. The formal opening session is at ten tomorrow morning with a buffet breakfast preceding it. Your parents are welcome to attend that session and the breakfast. Remember to check out in this room before you leave. Do you have any questions?"

"How do my parents find the Marriott?"

"It's just across campus. When they sign in at the parents' registration desk over there, they'll be given a map. Here's my card. I work in Admissions. If you have any questions now or later, contact me. Have a great time."

"Do you want to come with us while we register, or do you want to find your host?" her mom asked Katie.

"Umm, I guess I'll go over to the food lounge and see if she's there yet."

"Don't forget to pick up your suitcase in that room where we left them. When will we see you?" her mom added looking worried.

"I don't know, maybe tomorrow at the opening session? You can always call my cell," she said as she started to walk in the direction of the arrow that pointed to the food lounge.

"Have a good time," her dad called as she turned away.

Katie went into the lounge and was greeted by a student who told her he had signed up for this job because he enjoyed meeting all the prospective freshmen, that he remembered when he'd been admitted and come to preview weekend. "What's your name? I can check to see if your host has signed in." With a few clicks on a computer, he was able to tell Katie that her host was there. He sent a text message to Elizabeth.

Almost instantly, she came to the area where Katie was standing. "Hi, I'm Elizabeth. You must be Katie. How was your flight?" she asked as she extended her hand.

"Hi. The flight was fine," Katie said as she shook Elizabeth's hand.

"Did your parents come with you?"

"Yes. They're in the parents' registration area. They're staying at the Marriott."

"If you don't need to see them again today, we can pick up your bag and head over to the dorm."

"Sounds good," Katie said as they walked out the door toward the baggage area. They heard singing begin in the room where Katie and her parents had registered.

"Let's find out what's going on," Elizabeth said changing direction. The men's acappella group, the Beelzebubs, began singing one of their signature tunes. In less than a minute, everyone in the vicinity crowded around to enjoy the serenade. The Beelzebubs were well known on campus for their theatrical antics and her boyfriend was part of the group, Elizabeth told Katie. Katie saw Elizabeth give him a wave. Her boyfriend broke into a solo performance that wound up with the group surrounding Elizabeth and Katie.

After the singing ended, Elizabeth's boyfriend asked them how they liked the song. Before answering his question, Elizabeth introduced Katie. While Elizabeth and her boyfriend were talking, someone standing near Katie spoke to her.

"Hi, Katie. We met when you signed in. I'm Allie Lobelle.

"Hi."

"Is Beacon one of your top choices?"

"Yes. I'm hoping to figure out if I fit in during the weekend. My folks think it's a little far from home, but they'll be okay if I decide to come here. They've gone over to the Marriott."

"Preview weekend seems to work pretty well. Almost everyone has a good time and pre-frosh have a chance to find out if this is the place for him or her. I wish I could talk more with you, but it looks like another busload has arrived. I need to get back to the reception desk. I hope to see you on campus," Allie said.

Elizabeth and Katie continued their walk to the dorm. Katie wasn't sure what to talk about, but she didn't need to worry because Elizabeth was full of questions and comments. Elizabeth wanted to know what Katie's high school was like, what she wanted to major in, whether she had brothers or sisters. She told Katie she was one of five children and had a hard time imagining what it would be like to be an only child. Katie almost told her that her birth mother was from Massachusetts but didn't. Elizabeth unlocked the door to her room, pointed out the mattress on the floor with blankets and pillow where Katie would sleep, and showed her the bathroom shared with three other rooms. As Katie started to unpack, Elizabeth said she had to go to lab. Her friend, Emily, who lived down the hall, would be coming by to show Katie around campus.

After Elizabeth left, Katie felt a little

abandoned. She sat down on a desk chair and opened the preview program. She'd gotten to page three when there was a knock on the door and a voice asked, "Katie? Are you in?" The door opened a bit. "Hi. I'm Elizabeth's friend, Emily. I've come to take you on a tour of my favorite places. Ready?"

"Sure," Katie said as she put her shoes and coat back on. "Will I need anything?"

"It's a good idea to keep your wallet with you, even if you don't think you'll need it. Let's go. I've got lots of places to show you."

By the time they got to the bottom of the stairs, Emily had introduced Katie to three people who made her think enrolling would be a good decision. Then they ran into someone who told her he thought the faculty gave too much homework. He'd already spent three hours on his math problem sets that day, was nowhere near finished, and had to turn them in tomorrow. After he walked away, Emily pointed out that the homework was assigned a week ahead of time and that he probably shouldn't have started the day before. They continued on their exploration of the campus.

The first stop was back to the student center that Katie had briefly seen when she registered. Food was the most frequent item sought and found there. Burritos, pizzas, pressed sandwiches, Chinese dumplings, Tosci's homemade ice cream, and lots of coffee. Emily said that at Sunday brunch someone played the harp. They stopped at Tosci's where each ordered a single cone of

Very Berry sorbet. Emily suggested they sit in the comfortable chairs near the floor to ceiling windows where they could watch the comings and goings outside, almost as if they were in a movie theatre. Emily kept up a running commentary on what she thought was going on and who was headed where. Katie was glad not to talk much and have the chance to take it all in.

During the next two days, the campus was a three-ring circus with something for everyone. Some of the prefrosh attended classes, others avoided the classes and hung out with their hosts and friends. Was this what it was like to be a student here? Katie wondered. Probably not, or at least not most of the time, she thought. All the classes, the studying, the reading, the preparing for tests, all of that was missing, but everyone knew that. No matter at what college the students enrolled, they would have to study and pass their classes. What seemed more important, she thought, was to get a feel for the creative, fun aspects of the place. If it wasn't fun during preview, it wasn't likely to be fun at any time. How much she enjoyed the weekend was as good a way as any to choose a college as any, she thought.

When the weekend ended and the Lorkos were back at the airport for their flight to Chicago, they were happy they'd come; they'd learned a lot about Beacon and the area, but they were glad to be going home to sort out all the information.

On the plane, Katie's mom told her that she and her dad had gone to a financial aid session. Her dad said that many of the parents wanted to know if there was any way to reduce what they were expected to pay. They'd read a newspaper story that they should challenge the financial aid awards they had been offered in order to get a better result. He thought the financial aid people tried to be helpful, even if they couldn't reduce the amount the family was expected to pay at all, or by very much.

Katie hoped her parents would find a way to make the money numbers work. She knew they didn't want her to graduate from college with a lot of loan debt, but intended to use their savings, cut back on their expenses, and borrow the rest, though they felt they should not borrow against their retirement accounts. They'd heard stories of parents doing that and then having no way to finance a reasonable life style when they retired. They would find a way, even if it meant no vacations, new clothes, home improvements, or eating out much, for the next few years.

Over the next few weeks, Katie visited U of I again and a few other local colleges where she'd been admitted. She had a good time, but her heart belonged to Beacon. Her parents seemed resigned to the idea that she'd be moving a thousand miles away and that they'd have to borrow money. They went out to dinner at their favorite Italian restaurant the evening Katie sent her reply indicating her decision to enroll. It was the beginning of new lives for all of them. They wanted to celebrate. After all, she was their only child and the first in their immediate family to go to a four-year college. When the host welcomed them, Katie's dad said, "It's a big night for us. Katie just decided where she's going to enroll in college next fall."

"Where are you planning to go?" Mr. Eramo asked Katie.

"I'm going to Beacon in Massachusetts."

"We're all excited even though she'll be a long way away," Katie's mom added.

"Beacon! That's wonderful. My cousin's son graduated from there and he's doing very well. Congratulations," he said as he led them to a booth. After they'd finished their veal parmesan, lasagna, and chicken Marsala and were wondering whether they were too full to order dessert, their waitress came over to the table with tiramisu for everyone with Mr. Eramo's compliments.

CHAPTER FIFTEEN

Marina's plane arrived in San Francisco in the early afternoon. The lobby at the convention hotel was filled with academics. "Marina is that you?" Peter Plank asked. "Why are you at a physics conference?"

"Oh! Hi, Peter. I was asked to give a pre-conference workshop on my self-fulfilling prophecy research, but not at the physics meeting. The psychology conference starts in a few days. My workshop is tomorrow. Are you presenting a paper at the physics meeting?" Marina couldn't believe her bad luck in running into Peter.

"My presentation was today. Nick!" Peter said to a man who approached him. "How have you been? Let me introduce a colleague of mine, Marina Dubrova, this is Nick Carrante."

Nice looking; I wonder how he knows Peter, Marina thought, while explaining again that she was not attending the physics meeting. Nick asked if they would like to have dinner at a new restaurant not far from the hotel.

"I really can't, I have so much to do and…"

"I won't take no for an answer," Nick interrupted. "It won't be a long night. We'll be back in plenty of time for you to get ready for tomorrow's workshop. Meet you here in the lobby around seven?"

Marina excused herself and left the two men talking. Riding up in the elevator, all she could think was what a way to begin her time at her conference—having dinner with Peter Plank. At least we'll be in a good restaurant and Nick seems nice.

"Hi. It's pretty foggy out there," Marina said as she approached Nick in the lobby several hours later.

"Just a typical San Francisco night," he said smiling at her. "I'm looking forward to trying the restaurant and talking with you too. I've known Peter a long time so I'm glad to see him, but it's a lot better having someone like you along."

"I'm not sure Peter would share your sentiments."

"What do you mean? Oh. Hi, Peter. Ready to get going?"

Walking the few blocks uphill to the small French bistro not far from Union Square, Marina noticed when Nick's arm brushed hers.

Marina took the seat in between the two men in the restaurant.

"Are we all going to have wine?" Nick

asked.

"I don't drink much, but I'll have a glass," Peter said.

"How about starting with some Pinot Grigio? " Nick asked.

After selecting their dinner choices: salmon for Peter, veal for Marina, and duck for Nick, as well as a bottle of Pinot Noir to follow the Pinot Grigio, Peter asked Marina, "What will your workshop cover?"

"I'm going to discuss some of the ways that people who teach can use the ideas from my research to enhance their students' academic outcomes." She went on to describe what her studies had shown.

"I can't believe that just knowing you're part of an elite group can somehow influence your achievement," Peter said.

Before she could respond, she felt Nick's leg press against hers under the table. Rather than the pointed response at the tip of her tongue, she said only, "Well, I don't know what to say, except that believing you're considered above average can result in becoming just that."

With Nick's attentive interventions, the meal went smoothly. After they'd paid the bill and walked back to the hotel, he asked if they'd like to go into the bar to continue their conversation. "I have an early morning meeting, so I need to get to bed," Peter said as he left to go to the elevators.

Marina and Nick went into the hotel bar and ordered champagne. Nick looked at

Marina and said he knew Peter could be a pain at times. "I hope you don't think all physicists are like him."

"No, of course not. He seems to rub me the wrong way. I guess it's because there's some history." She quietly told Nick about Peter's voting against her for tenure.

"That's why tenure votes should be kept secret. Bad feelings can last a long time. Peter caused the discussion about your research on the Pygmalion effect to be cut short. I'd like to hear more."

After telling Nick about the funding she had received in the past, Marina felt more relaxed than she had in a while. "I'm thinking about trying my theories out on people who don't know they're in an experiment." She told him about her project with the Admissions Office, that it was confidential, and then said, "I better go to bed. I'm so tired."

In the elevator, Nick asked Marina if she'd like to have a quick nightcap in his room.

"That sounds good, but I have to get to sleep because my workshop is tomorrow morning."

Nick said he was disappointed. Maybe they could catch up the next afternoon.

In the morning, Marina woke up early. She was still on East Coast time. She put on her swimsuit, yoga pants, and sweatshirt and took the elevator down to the pool.

A few people were swimming back and forth as if they were in lanes. She thought one of the swimmers looked like Nick, but without her contacts she had a hard time deciding. She found a chair and dropped her pool towel and clothes onto it. She felt good in her bathing suit, black with a deep V-neck top. When she turned to face the pool, Nick swam up to the edge. "The water's warm. Come in."

"I don't like to get wet all at once. I'm going down to the shallow end."

Nick met her there. "Don't splash me. I need a minute." Marina took steps forward and then ducked below the water to get her hair wet. She started swimming to the far end. They both did easy laps for about ten minutes, then Nick caught Marina's ankle. "Let's go sit in the whirlpool. I'm interested in learning more about your research."

"Okay, but just for a few minutes. I need to get some breakfast before my workshop." Fifteen minutes later they left for the coffee shop. Marina ate quickly and left to dress for her meeting. Nick said he'd try to meet her later.

After the workshop ended, Marina sat down in the hotel lobby in a high-backed upholstered chair to review the conference program. Behind her, she heard Nick's and Peter's voices. Before she could stand up to say hello, she heard Nick say, "Marina and I had a drink last night after you left. She's doing some interesting research with the Admissions Office. Maybe you know about it?"

Peter sounded surprised and said he didn't know.

"I need to leave earlier than I expected. If you see Marina, would you tell her goodbye for me?" They walked away.

I can't believe Nick would tell Peter about the experiment. I thought he liked me. Maybe I didn't make it clear enough that it was a big secret. I never should have agreed to get involved with Max's project, especially when he couldn't even get Skinner to let us admit as many specials as I thought we needed. I hope this doesn't cause any trouble for Max, but if it does, I'm sure he'll be able to handle it.

After the conference ended and she returned to Boston, the freshmen, including the special admits, had started arriving for orientation. Marina didn't know whether to tell Max that Peter knew about the experiment. Peter is sure to tell other faculty, she thought. He probably already has. When she called Max's office number, a recording said that he was out for a few days. I'm not sure I want to talk to him anyway, she thought as she hung up.

———————

After Nick Carrante talked to Peter about Marina's Pygmalion research that involved the freshman class and the Admissions Dean, Peter couldn't stop thinking about it. He ran into someone from his department at the conference and asked him what he thought of the freshmen. His colleague said he thought they were okay, but that they weren't as strong as they used to be. "Do you think Admissions could do a better job?" Peter asked.

"I don't know. Probably. The Dean doesn't seem as good a fit for Beacon's culture as the previous one was. Maybe he doesn't understand what kind of students we need."

Peter wanted to find out if Marina's research involving the Admissions Office was ethical and in fact if the president knew about it. He didn't want Beacon to be cast in a bad light so he'd have to be careful about whom he talked to.

After he returned from the physics conference, Peter made an appointment to see Max. When they were together in Max's office, he said that he'd heard that some freshmen had been admitted without fully evaluating their extracurricular activities and that Max and Marina were engaged in an experiment. Before he brought the matter up with anyone else, he wanted to give Max a chance to explain why he would do something so crazy.

Max, caught off guard, said he'd be right back; he needed to tell Natalie something. Outside of his office, Max wondered how Peter found out. Should I tell him that Skinner knows?

After thinking his options through, Max returned, said he hoped that Peter, a scientist, would understand that he and Marina had seen an opportunity to test the value of considering whether a match between the interests of the applicants and the culture of the university was important for the freshmen's success. He went on to explain that many applicants had good grades and scores and could be appropriate choices, but admissions staff felt that students would do better if their interests were consistent with Beacon's values. Alternatively, Marina's research had shown that the match might be less important than the fact that the applicant had been admitted to a prestigious college. Those admitted would rise to the occasion, she believed.

Max kept talking and talking until Peter said, "Wait a minute. When you chose those who would be admitted without a full read, did you at least check to see if their grades and scores were good enough? Not just good enough, but very good?"

"Only those who had a good chance of being admitted get triaged in, selected, for a full read. We picked the special admits from that group without doing the second read."

"I guess if these special admits do well, there won't be a need to spend so much time reading all the essays and bothering to think about the types of activities the applicants have. We might even be able to save money by reducing the size of the admissions staff," Peter said.

Peter probably thought he could curry

favor with the trustees by finding ways to reduce costs, Max thought.

"Well I'm glad we got that cleared up," Peter said. "This so-called experiment might finally allow us to focus on the things that are important."

Alone again, Max called Marina. "Peter Plank was just here. Did you tell him about our project?"

Marina said no, but she had told someone else who might have told Peter. She didn't think it was important. "Is there a problem?"

"I wasn't happy that Peter asked me if my staff had admitted some freshmen without carefully reading their applications."

"Don't worry. Everything will be okay. I have to run."

If Marina is right that the match isn't that important, but these admits feel special having been admitted to a prestigious college, the specials should do fine; if she's wrong about her theory, they may not do as well. Given they're good enough academically, with the help available from tutoring and the special counseling and advising staff that Skinner has funded, the specials should do okay once they adjust Max thought, that is, unless the match is as important as Admissions staff think. Even so, he did not feel secure knowing that Peter, of all people, knew about the experiment.

CHAPTER SIXTEEN

After Allie met Katie at campus preview weekend, she regularly checked the database to see if Katie planned to enroll. Finally, her reply indicating that she would enroll turned up on May third.

Over the summer months, while she was catching up on all the research projects she needed to finish, as well as planning her fall recruitment travel and taking a vacation to Provincetown with her husband and daughter, Allie thought about how much she wanted to talk to Katie about Paula Kotski. However, September came and the freshmen arrived on campus. Allie didn't feel comfortable with any approach to the conversation she could imagine having with Katie. On the first of October, she left for fall admissions travel.

When Allie returned in mid-October, she felt as if she had a million things to finish before the reading season began in early November. After spending a week catching up at the office as well as at home, she decided it would not be appropriate to talk with Katie without the Lorkos' permission.

Instead of telephoning them, she wrote a letter describing what she knew about Katie's past, including her own relationship with Katie's birth mother, Paula. At the end of October, she mailed the letter on white paper without Beacon's logo, in a plain envelope with her own first and last name and home address written in ink on the back.

About a week later, a response came from the Carolyn and Paul Lorko saying they'd been surprised to receive her letter, but after speaking with their daughter, they were willing to have her talk with Katie.

At work the next day, Allie called Katie's advisor, Professor Lydia Moroney to ask if she could come over and talk to her. Lydia and Allie had grown friendly while serving on the university's student grade review committee. "I'm working on my next class lecture, but I can take a break and meet you in the café on the first floor." Allie put on her coat and walked out the office door without speaking to anyone. Before she talked to Lydia, she had to think through one last time how to tell Katie's story as well as how to approach Katie herself. She'd told the Lorkos that she would talk to Katie in her advisor's presence, and maybe at some later time take her out to the town, Laketon, where she and Paula Kotski had grown up.

When she got to the café, Lydia was already sitting at a corner table drinking coffee and reading something on her iPad. Allie went over to the counter, bought herself a black coffee, and quickly sat down with Lydia. After exchanging the usual greetings and comments about the weather and work, Allie got right to the point. "I want to run something by you. It involves your advisee, Katie Lorko. Nothing's wrong," she quickly added as Lydia's eyes took on an alarmed look. "It's kind of a long story, but I'll try to make it short. You know Katie is adopted. What you don't know is her birth mother, Paula Kotski, and I were best friends in high school."

"Really? That's interesting and not what I expected you to talk about," Lydia said. "But go on, sorry for interrupting."

"I'll give you the short version. Paula got pregnant in graduate school. She wasn't married and decided to live with her cousin in Illinois until she had the baby. That's Katie. The Lorkos adopted her. My friend, who later married someone not Katie's father, was travelling back from a Vermont ski trip about ten years ago, when another car crossed the median. Paula, her husband, and son were all killed. Katie's grandfather was already dead by that time. Her grandmother, Paula's mother, is in a nursing home with dementia. I wrote to the Lorkos asking their permission to speak to Katie. They talked with her and all agreed it's okay for me to meet with her. I'd like to do it in your office. I'll tell her about my relationship with Paula and the Kotski family. Would you be willing and how do you think she'll take it?"

"I'm sure Katie would like to learn about

Paula and your relationship with her. You don't want her to feel insecure about why she was admitted though. You know how some freshmen can be, wondering whether they're here because of a mistake. She seems grounded and is doing okay, but probably not as well as she'd hoped. I don't think she'll have any trouble in the long run, but it takes time to get adjusted. Why don't I set up a meeting with her so that you can meet here in my office and I can help if I'm needed?"

"I hoped you would do that," Allie said.

Katie, Dr. Moroney, and Allie met in early November after Allie had spent too much time thinking about how she would tell Katie about the Kotski's. After she and Katie were reintroduced by Lydia, Katie admitted she didn't remember meeting Allie at campus preview. Lydia brought them both tea. Allie said, "Your folks told you I want to talk to you about your birth mother, Paula Kotski. She was my best friend in high school and even before. I've wanted to tell you that, what she was like, and about her family ever since I knew you were enrolling. In her letter, your mother said they told you about Paula's death a few years ago. I brought along a few pictures, mostly of Paula and me when we were in high school. Let me get them out of my pocketbook." Allie pulled them out, and then spread them across the coffee table so all of them could see.

Before the pictures, Katie had been reserved, but once she saw Paula, who had the same hair color as she did, she became eager to hear about the family she'd never known. The hair connection seemed to open up the channels that allowed her to ask many questions, including, "Do you know why she gave me up? What color eyes did Paula have? Do I look like her? Did you know my father?"

The last question was the only one Allie hadn't thought about before. She told Katie that Paula did not inform him about her pregnancy. Their relationship wasn't long standing. "She didn't tell him she was pregnant?"

"No, she didn't and I don't really know why except she didn't feel he was the right person to marry. I wish I knew more but I don't." She saw Katie's eyes fill with tears. She realized she had never quite seen Paula's behavior from Katie's point of view. "All I can say is that times were different from the way they are now and it was more difficult for a woman to raise a child by herself without a partner. You make me realize there are many things I never asked about."

When Katie regained her composure, she told Allie that her mother had almost not opened Allie's letter, that she often threw mail unopened into the wastebasket if it looked like junk mail, but the return address in Massachusetts, as well as the full postage, caused her to open the letter and then hardly believe what she was reading. Katie said her mom told her she thought at first it might be a bad joke, but she knew it wasn't, and that her mother had felt insecure in earlier years, thinking maybe Katie would like Paula better than she liked her.

Katie said both of her parents' felt that Allie sounded normal, that it was a surprise that she worked in the Admissions Office. They knew it was natural for Katie to want to know more about her birth family, but were worried how it would affect her since she'd just started college and needed to keep her mind on her studies. Her parents had spent the weekend discussing what to do and finally called her to ask if she was interested in having Allie contact her. If she was, that's what they'd put in their letter; if not, then that's what they'd say.

"I said my birth mother's friend works in the Admissions Office here? I couldn't believe it. I asked them if they thought that's why I was admitted. They didn't think so. I told them it was okay for you to contact me. I guess I want to find out what my mother and her family were like."

"First of all, I didn't make the decision to admit you. Other Admissions staff did. Maybe in the spring when you have a free day, we could drive out to Laketon. I can show you some of the places where Paula and I hung out including the high school."

The time had gone by so quickly that Katie, looking at her phone, exclaimed that her biology lab was about to start and she had to run. "I guess I'd like to go with you to Laketon if it works out."

"If you have any questions, email or text me, call, or stop by the office. I'm so glad you decided to enroll here," Allie said.

Allie and Lydia spent a few minutes going over how they thought Katie had received the information—about as well as they could have hoped, they thought.

As Katie rushed to her class, she felt both exhilarated by what she'd heard and seen, and also very sad because she hadn't learned more about why Paula had given her up for adoption or who her birth father was. She didn't want to talk to her mom about all of this. As she pushed open the glass doors that led to the hallway near her classroom, she noticed a large yellow sign announcing expanded hours for the counseling office. Maybe that's where I need to go, she thought. I'm so mixed up.

CHAPTER SEVENTEEN

The previous spring when Marina told Sue a subset of freshmen had been admitted slightly differently from the others, Sue wanted to ask what the difference was, but felt Marina didn't want to discuss that. She knew she needed to examine whether the two groups differed in their first semester grade point averages and probably again later, after they had finished their freshman year.

Sue and her counterpart in the Registrar's Office figured out a way to organize the data so that Sue and Marina would not know the individual identities of the students in either the experimental (Group 1) or control group (Group 2). Now, months after that initial discussion with Marina, the freshmen had completed their first semester and Sue had received their data, including course grades, number of credits taken, number of courses dropped, and so on, and began to work on getting the data ready for analysis.

Marina came by to talk about how the analysis was going. "I think I'll have some basic information in a couple of days," Sue said. "I've done the merge of our data with that from the Registrar, and made a copy in which I've hidden the identifying information. It'll take me awhile to run some basic frequencies and make any corrections that are needed."

"Sounds good. If you need help thinking through the analyses, let me know. I'm anxious to find out how the students in those two groups did. Call me when you've got something," Marina said as she left.

The semester break that started before the Christmas holidays was still on and many grad students were away or taking a relaxed approach to their work. Sue decided to go to the gym before lunch. Her mother was always telling her she should exercise more: Pilates this, Pilates that. One of Sue's New Year's resolutions was to go to the gym three times a week. She might even look into the schedule to see if a Pilates class was given at a convenient time. Most of the grad students she knew were like her. They spent a lot of time working on the research projects of their faculty advisors, teaching intro courses or sections, and working on their dissertations or studying for comprehensive exams. Even if they weren't actively writing, doing research, or studying, they felt they should be and that felt like work. They talked to each other about what they wanted to do when they completed their graduate studies, but didn't spend much time at the gym. Sue had been there enough, though, not to feel uncomfortable.

After pulling her long brown hair into a ponytail, she set the timer on the elliptical machine for thirty minutes. After the time was up, she continued exercising on what she thought of as the chip and dip machine. She could not remember its name, but she knelt on a pad and either hauled herself up or pushed herself down. The feeling of movement, of flying almost, was the best thing. She had a recurring fantasy that if she let go at the right moment, she could vault herself over the top and land on the wrestling mats below.

After finishing her set, Sue headed toward the locker room and almost collided with John, another graduate student in the psychology department, who was coming around the corner from the men's locker room. "Are you leaving?" he asked.

"I'm done. How long have you been back? Didn't you go home for Christmas?"

"I flew in last night. It was so cold in Chicago that this place seems tropical. Tom, Monica, Kirsten, Mike, and Ben want to go for pizza tonight. Are you interested?"

"Sure. I'll be working in my office this afternoon. What time should I meet you?" She was pleased to be included and especially by John. They'd started talking toward the end of last semester. She wouldn't mind getting to know him better. He was a year ahead of her in the social psychology program and expected, or at least hoped, to finish that spring. He'd told her he was already looking for a postdoc.

"I'll come by and get you around six thirty," he said as he walked toward the main gym.

"Okay." She walked toward the entrance of the women's locker room and then straight ahead to her locker in the fourth row. Well, that's good, she thought. Tom, Monica, Kirsten, and Mike were friends of hers. She'd met Ben, but wasn't sure what he was like. At least she wouldn't have to worry about making dinner. Since classes hadn't started yet for the semester, she felt she deserved a break. After the semester began, she knew she would have less time for social events and would spend most of her time working for Marina or on her dissertation proposal. She needed to be more focused if she expected to finish her PhD in a few years.

After she returned to her office and finished eating lunch, Sue opened Marina's file and started running frequencies on the data. All the numbers looked okay; nothing seemed unusual. Marina had told her to compare the grade point averages of the students in Group 1, the experimental group, with those in Group 2, the control group. Before that, she ran a different statistical test on the data, specifically on gender, and found the number of men and women in each group was as expected, about the same. The statistical test to examine whether the mean grade point average in Group 1 was different from the mean grade point average in Group

2 was the t-test. The test showed a difference between the groups so the treatment could have been responsible. In other words, the mean grade point average of Group 1 was not the same as the mean grade point average of Group 2 at the end of the first semester. That might make Marina happy she hoped.

The phone rang. When she picked it up, Patti from the Registrar's Office was on the line.

"Hey, Sue. I got some more data for the freshmen, so I'm sending you another file. How's it going?"

"Okay. Will you be sending me a lot more data?"

"I don't know. I thought I'd given you everything the last time, but later I was told I should send you this information about the number of times the students had contacted the Dean's Office. Let me know if it doesn't look right," Patti said as she hung up.

Fine, if it's like the other data, maybe there will be some difference, Sue thought. The file with the new data from Patti popped up in her email. She spent the next couple of hours getting it organized and adding it to the data she already had.

She'd just finished when she realized it was almost time for John to come for her. She closed the computer, put it into her backpack, and locked the door since she was the only one left then walked down the hall to join the others.

The next morning she had a headache

probably from too many beers. They'd spent hours talking, eating pizza, and drinking at Mary Ann's. They complained about working for faculty who took them for granted.

Well, she didn't have time to think about that. Her meeting with Marina was at eleven so she had to get moving or she'd be late. She grabbed her backpack, said goodbye to the cat, ran out the door, and jumped into her freezing cold Honda Civic. At least she didn't have to walk to the 'T'. One good thing about working for Marina was that her parking permit was paid for by Marina's grant.

She parked and walked over to McGuinn Hall. On the third floor she checked her department mailbox and found a flyer reminding everyone to come to a seminar next week. The department secretary asked her if she'd seen Marina yet because someone from Admissions had called asking for her. "I haven't seen her yet," Sue said. "I'll mention the call when I meet with her." Back in her office, Sue picked up the printouts of the data she'd been working on the day before along with her notebook and pen. It was eleven now, so she walked over to Marina's office and knocked on the door.

"Come in."

"Hi, Marina. I've brought the output. Are you ready to talk about it?"

"Yes, I'm ready. Max Danker from the Admissions Office is going to join us. Have you met him?" Marina asked.

"No. Is he the Dean?"

"Yes, the project you're working on is something he's interested in. You have to keep that confidential though."

"What is he…" Sue started to say when there was a knock on the door before it opened.

"Hi, Max. Come in. I was just talking to Sue Butler, my research assistant, who's working on the data," Marina said.

"Hi, Sue. Nice to meet you," he said and extended his hand.

"Nice to meet you, too."

"What results do you have?" Marina asked after they'd all sat down.

"Well, statistically the two groups are slightly different as far as their grade point averages goes. The probability is equal to or less than .05 that the means are actually the same. Group 1 has a mean GPA of 2.6 for the first semester and Group 2 has a mean of 2.8. Is that sort of what you were expecting?" Sue asked.

"Which group is the experimental one?" Marina asked.

"Group 2 is the one you said to call the control group. The one you said to call the experimental group, Group 1, has the lower GPA, the 2.6."

"Are you sure?" Max asked. His face looked flushed to Sue.

"I'm pretty sure. I got the data file from the Registrar's Office and merged it with data Marina gave me. It was straightforward. I can't see any way that it wouldn't be right,"

Sue said as Max's cell phone began to ring.

He looked at the caller's number and said, "I need to get back to my office. Can you look at the data again and make sure there isn't any mistake? This is very important. Will you call me as soon as you've checked?" Max asked as he hurried toward the door.

"I'll redo all the steps and make sure I didn't do anything wrong. I don't think I did. I guess he didn't like the results," she said to Marina after the door shut.

"Let me know after you've redone the statistics. Make sure you start from the beginning. Remerge the data and all that," Marina said as Sue was gathering her printouts and notes.

Sue went back to her office and shut the door. I wish I knew what they were looking for. It's not like Marina to be so secretive. After I eat lunch, I'll redo all the data, she thought to herself as she took a couple of ibuprofen and headed down the hall toward the community refrigerator to retrieve her yogurt.

"Hey, Sue. I had a good time last night. How about you?" Monica asked.

"I did, but I have a splitting headache. Probably my own fault," Sue replied as she foraged in the refrigerator for the lunch bag on which her name was written in black magic marker. Last year someone kept taking her lunch, so this year she made sure she wrote her name on the bag in super size letters. So far no one had "mistakenly" taken her food.

"Here let me help you with a relaxation technique I learned at a class I took."

"I don't have time. I've got to redo a bunch of data for Marina."

"This won't take long and you'll feel a lot better. Sit here," Monica commanded.

"Oh, okay. I'm not in very good shape to work anyway," Sue conceded.

Monica proceeded to explain and then lead Sue through the relaxation techniques she'd learned. "That helps. I'm glad you talked me into it. Where did you learn to do it?"

"The grad dean's office had a workshop a few weeks ago. Anyone could go. Not many people were there, but it was great. We should take advantage of all the things this place offers. It wouldn't be half bad to be a student here if we did more of the fun stuff."

After about five minutes, Sue said, "You know, I think my headache's gone. What can I do for you?"

"Nothing. I'm glad I could help. If you want to come with us for sushi tonight, we'll probably be going. Want me to pick you up if we decide to go?"

"Sure. I'll be here all afternoon redoing these statistics," Sue said as she got up, picked up her yogurt, and headed for the door.

Okay, now I have to get down to business, Sue thought. She opened her laptop, and checked her Facebook account. She had five new messages so she read and responded to them. When she looked for the files from the Registrar and from Marina to merge again, she couldn't find the one from the Registrar. It had been on her desktop and now it just wasn't there. It wasn't in the recycle bin on her computer either. Did she need to call Patti and ask her to resend the data? Maybe she still had the email that Patti had sent her with the data file as an attachment. Then she remembered she'd put the data in a folder called, "Keep." There it was, praise the Lord, she thought. She needed a cup of tea to get through the rest of the afternoon.

In the office at the hot/cold water station, she ran into John.

"Are you coming with us for sushi tonight?" he asked.

"I'm planning to, but I have to finish this stuff for Marina," Sue said as she filled her cup with hot water and then added a tea bag from the box on the counter.

"Your work will still be here tomorrow. We're not going to leave until about seven, so you have a couple of hours to finish. What are you doing anyway?"

"It's a project for Marina. I don't know a lot about it. I just have to run statistical tests. It's some kind of experiment and whether the treatment makes any difference in the grades students get."

"Is Marina still doing research on how people do what's expected of them, the Pygmalion thing?"

"I think so. She hasn't really told me what this is about, but I know the Admissions Office is interested in it," Sue said, then immediately realized she shouldn't have mentioned the Admissions Office.

"The Admissions Office? Why are they involved?" John asked.

"I really don't know any more than that. I have to run. See you later," she said as she escaped out the door and walked down the hall toward her office. Now why did I have to tell him that? I don't have enough trouble. Marina told me not to mention Admissions. I've wasted enough time. I'd better redo the statistics or I won't be able to go out for dinner.

After she merged the data and reran the numbers, the results were the same. The experimental group had not done as well as the control. Just as she figured this out, John opened Sue's door and said, "Ready to go? Everybody's waiting in the main office."

"I really shouldn't go. I need to finish this stuff before tomorrow," Sue said while simultaneously shutting her computer down and reaching for her coat and backpack. After she put her computer into her backpack, she said, "I shouldn't, but I will. Life is too short to waste on statistics. I have my car. Should I follow you guys? Which restaurant are we going to?"

"I think we're all taking our own cars so we can go home directly from the restaurant. We thought we'd go to Everything Sushi. Is that okay with you?"

"Sure," Sue said as she followed John into the main office where Monica and the others were waiting.

The battery in her cell phone was dead so she threw it into her backpack in the trunk of her car. Sue drove toward the exit where she found herself in a line with the others in their Hondas, Toyotas, and Fords with the garage attendant standing near the machine that usually operated the gate automatically. The machine had frequent problems and Sue wound up in this kind of backup more often than she liked. The garage guy was very nice and tried to get them out quickly, but it all took time. At least she could file her nails with the emery board she kept in the car's glove compartment. She felt better when she didn't waste time she told herself.

Even though they all planned to make it an early night after they'd been out late the night before, someone, probably Ben, suggested they go over to his apartment and watch one of those chef challenge programs. For some reason they all thought this was a great idea. Once there, they drank a lot of Carlo Rossi wine and talked even more about all the work they had. Monica did more relaxation exercises and Sue and everyone else wound up leaving their cars and taking cabs home. Fortunately, Sue didn't live far away and her share of the cab ride was only five dollars. She planned to walk over in the morning to rescue her car.

It couldn't be morning already, she thought as she turned over and noticed the clock said seven fifteen as she shut off the alarm. She closed her eyes just for a minute and when she looked at the clock again, it said eight thirty. Now she'd have to rush. Marina would be knocking on her office door. She'd probably call her on her cell at any moment. She'd better find her phone. Where was it? Oh, no. It was in the backpack in the trunk of the car. She hurried through her morning routine and ended it by saying goodbye to the cat. Only when she went outside and looked for her car did she remember the car was parked near Ben's apartment.

There was nothing to do but start walking. Her boots were comfortable. She had on her down jacket, Lands End hat, warm gloves, and a long fuzzy red scarf. She found the car, took her cell phone out of the backpack and plugged it into the car charger. One of the missed calls was from Marina. Another was from Max. Rather than listen to the voicemails, she started the car and began to drive toward Beacon. She'd stop at Marina's office when she got to McGuinn. The parking garage had the all too familiar line at the entrance. The garage attendant was waving people in and answering the questions of visitors who hadn't a clue where they should park. Finally, she got into the garage, drove to the basement, parked, and fast walked to her building.

She dropped off her coat, opened her computer, and printed the results out. She knocked on Marina's door, and then opened it. Marina was on the phone, but motioned for her to come in and sit down.

"She just came in. I'll call you after we've talked," Marina said as she put down the phone. "Have you had a chance to take another look at the data? That was Max. He said he couldn't reach you last night."

"When I redid the statistics, the results were the same: the control group did better than the experimental one."

"You're sure? I have a committee meeting in two minutes, but I have to call Max and tell him. Can you draft the results and send them to me as an email attachment by noon?" Marina asked.

Marina was tapping numbers into her phone. Sue went to her office, grabbed her cup, and walked down the hall to the coffee station. The office assistant was pouring the last drop into her cup.

"Hi, Sue. How's it going? Marina on your case? I just used up the coffee, but I'll make another pot."

"Thanks. You know how it is. Everything has to be done yesterday. But it's okay. Once I have coffee, I'll be fine." The room smelled good, she thought. Coffee, especially in the morning, was absolutely the right thing. She couldn't understand how some people didn't like it or preferred tea. She liked tea in the afternoon, but only after having coffee in the morning. The assistant poured water into the coffee machine and popped a pre-filled coffee filter into the basket. After a few minutes, Sue poured herself a cup and then walked down the hall toward her own office where she found her office mate already working on his computer. "You're here bright and early," Sue said.

"I have to get this done. My advisor is worried that we'll lose our funding if we don't get the report in right away. Just pretend I'm not here."

"I've got stuff to do too." Sue typed a narrative of what she thought the data showed. The freshmen in Group 1, the experimental, and those in Group 2, the control, were statistically different in terms of their grade point averages at the end of the first semester. Next, she reported the percentage of freshmen in each group who had contacted the Dean's Office to express an interest in transferring out of Beacon into some other college. She had not had time to look at that aspect of the data before she met with Marina, and found that a statistically higher percentage of freshmen in Group 1 had expressed an interest in transferring out. Sue didn't know whether Marina would see these new findings as good or bad.

Before lunch, when she had finished the draft, Sue sent the report to Marina as an email attachment. She shut off her computer, walked down to the room with the refrigerator, and took out her lunch bag. Just then Monica and Ben came into the office and took their lunches from the refrigerator. The three of them walked over to the grad student lounge and sat on the sofa near the television.

"I've finally finished the draft for Marina," Sue announced as they began eating yogurt and leftover pizza.

"What did you find?" Ben asked.

"The experimental group was not as good as the control."

"So the treatment had a negative effect?"

"Right, but I don't know what the treatment was."

"What happens next?" Monica asked.

"This is the first semester data. I have to redo it when next semester's over."

Meanwhile, Ben looked up and asked if they'd be interested in watching a DVD that night.

CHAPTER EIGHTEEN

Max left Marina's office worrying that the random admits had done poorly. He went straight to a meeting with Vincent Carr, the CAFA chair. "I've been hearing from alumni about the mostly good decisions you make," Vincent said. "Some of the faculty, though, are concerned that the freshmen seem less, what's the word, academically driven, than they used to be. I know you don't want to do anything to cause more discontent. I want to make sure our academic standards stay up there."

"I can give you a run down about the process."

"I'm not interested in details, but I have a concern. Yesterday, a faculty member called to ask if I'd heard anything about some kind of experiment with admissions. I told him I hadn't. Furthermore, I added that our Admissions Dean wouldn't do anything to put our reputation in jeopardy."

Max experienced an adrenalin jolt. "You're right. I'm probably the university's biggest cheerleader. I wouldn't do anything to make us look bad. I anticipate receiving a lot more applications next fall. Will you support my request for money to hire temporary readers? We'll have trouble keeping up without help."

"Why don't you talk to the president? He's on a trip right now, but see him when he gets back. He told me the trustees have set up a discretionary fund to be used by some offices including Admissions and Financial Services."

That night, Max couldn't reach Sue on her cell phone to find out if she'd reanalyzed the data. She wasn't answering. After tossing and turning for a while, he finally fell asleep. The telephone rang. He picked it up and heard someone say, "Max? Is that you? I've got terrible news. Chuck Skinner was in Hong Kong having dinner with some alums, he went into anaphylactic shock, and died before they could get him to the hospital. The chef, ignoring instructions that no nuts be used because of Chuck's allergy, purposely used peanut oil because he was angry that his son wasn't admitted to Beacon even though less qualified classmates were admitted. Peter Plank is interim president."

Max's eyes snapped open. He got out of bed feeling upset, even as the dream was fading from his mind. His job would become more difficult if the special admits had performed poorly last semester.

"Hi, Boss," Andy greeted him when he walked into the office. "How was your meeting with Vincent?"

"Okay. He told me the president has some discretionary money. "

Natalie walked over to tell Max that Professor Dubrova was anxious to have him return her call because of some project they were working on.

"The special admits didn't do as well as I expected they would last semester. Sue rechecked the results and they still didn't do as well as those admitted the traditional way," Marina said, "but…"

"I thought your theory predicted they would do as well," Max interrupted. "I wouldn't have agreed to do this experiment if you hadn't assured me that they'd do as well," Max said. "What will I tell people?"

"You don't have to say anything. I think when we look at their grades at the end of spring semester they will have caught up. The differences aren't very large even now. I have a class starting in a few minutes so I have to go. We can talk more later if you want."

Now what do I do? Max mused. Should I call the counseling office and tell them? I guess they will know soon enough if they don't already. Should I call Skinner? He has enough on his plate without this, and as Marina says, the specials should catch up by the end of spring semester—so I'll wait.

In February, the Admissions staff admitted the next class the traditional way. An article appeared in *The Spotlight* reporting an interview with one of the counseling deans who said their office had been busier with more freshmen seeking help, but the dean felt that was a good sign, that students weren't waiting as long as they had in the past. Max wondered whether anyone would call again to ask him if he'd admitted last fall's freshmen any differently. Peter Plank called to ask if the class they'd just admitted had been admitted the traditional way. Max told him they had been. Skinner called to ask if they planned to look at the spring semester grades of the freshmen. Max said they would and that Marina believed by the end of the second semester the grades of the specials would be more or less the same as those admitted the traditional way. His fingers, again, were crossed behind his back.

CHAPTER NINETEEN

When she was home for Thanksgiving, Katie and her parents talked about her meeting with Allie. "I couldn't believe someone at Beacon knew my birth mother. "Allie gave me these pictures. Do you think I look like her?"

"Maybe a little, especially the hair," her mom said.

"I wish I could show them to Dave, but he's visiting grandparents in Missouri. I don't know why he couldn't have spent at least a few hours with me before he left. I guess they had to leave before the traffic got worse." That weekend, Katie shopped with her mom, had lunch with a friend, and then flew back to Boston after an all too short break.

When she returned to college, it seemed as if she hardly had time to unpack before she was studying for finals. "When's your last exam?" she asked her roommate.

"On Thursday. My folks are coming to get me that afternoon. I don't know what I'd do if I couldn't put all my stuff in their car," Ruth Ann said. "I don't know how you do it."

When her exams were over, Katie packed her bags, took the subway to the airport, and flew to Chicago, ready to see her friends, eat her favorite foods, and especially hang out with Dave. "I worked so hard. I hope I get at least one A," she said to her parents when they met her at the airport. They told her that as long as she passed her courses, they would be pleased.

Thinking ahead to spring semester, Katie hoped she would deal with problems in a more mature way than she had last semester. She remembered how upset she'd been when an English paper came back with an enormous 'D' on it. She'd immediately run over to her advisor's office. "What's wrong?" Dr. Moroney asked when Katie walked in and started to cry. "Sit down. Let me get you a cup of tea. We can talk."

"No matter what I do, I can't get a better grade in English than a C."

"Have you tried studying with others from your class?" Dr. Moroney asked as she handed Katie her tea.

"No. I can talk to the girl who sits next to me and see if she's interested. Maybe she knows someone else."

"You could meet and read each other's essays before you hand them in."

After her next English class, Katie asked the person she sat next to if she was interested in forming a writing group. Julie was interested and thought another girl in the class would be too. They agreed to meet on the weekend and read each other's work.

After the semester was over and she was back home, Katie told her parents, "At first it was hard for me to let them see my writing and not feel nervous, but it was worth it. I didn't get an A, but at least I got a B. I hope I can do even better next semester. Did I tell you that I've gotten used to living with all of Ruth Ann's stuff? I can't believe how much she has. I guess it's because she doesn't live far away. I'm thinking of rooming with someone in my writing group next year."

Katie wanted especially to see Dave since he hadn't been around at Thanksgiving. Before leaving for college last September, Katie and Dave told each other they hoped they could keep up their relationship. They pledged to stay friendly no matter what happened. At college, Katie had male friends, but she hadn't found someone special and she didn't want to because she loved Dave. After exams, the night before she flew home, he had called. "Can we get together for dinner the first night you're back?"

They went to their favorite Chinese restaurant and ordered the usual things: dumplings, chicken with cashew nuts, moo-shi beef, same as always. "I study a lot, I think, but my grades aren't as good as I want," Katie said. "My writing group has made a difference. Maybe I need something like that for my other subjects." While she waited for Dave to respond, she noticed that he seemed a little different. He'd forgotten that they always ordered moo-shi beef and said they wanted moo-shi chicken until Katie corrected him. She guessed he was still recovering from finals.

"I feel the same way about some of my classes at Illinois," Dave said. When they were eating their fortune cookies, he was studying his fortune when he looked up and said, "I've met someone who reminds me a lot of you. She and I were in the same history class and we both liked to study in the library. Now we're kind of a couple. I won't be seeing her over the break because Sarah and her family are in California visiting grandparents." He hoped he and Katie could still be friends.

Katie couldn't believe what she'd heard. He'd met someone who looked like her, but who he liked better than her? "I thought we really liked each other?"

"I didn't mean for this to happen."

"Then why did it? I can't believe I trusted you. I went out with some people, but I knew I wasn't going to get involved with anyone. I thought you were different, not like all the others. You're such a jerk," Katie said and threw her fortune cookie in his face. "I want to go home." They paid the check, and then walked to the car.

"Katie, don't be like that. I still want to be friends with you."

"Forget it. You sure didn't lose any time."

When Dave tried to continue the

conversation, Katie refused to respond. They passed the rest of the ride in silence. When they reached her house, Katie didn't say goodbye, but jumped out, slammed the door, and raced up the front steps.

"Back so soon?" her mom called from the kitchen.

"Yeah, we're still pretty tired. I think I'll read for awhile and go to bed," Katie called from the front hall as she started up the stairs to her room.

She heard her dad come out of the den, walk toward the kitchen, and ask, "Do you think anything's wrong? Isn't she back awfully early?"

"I guess we'll find out eventually. Better not to ask," she heard her mom say.

I'll tell them tomorrow, Katie thought. Maybe it was a mistake to go to college in Boston. If I'd stayed in Illinois, we might still be together. When she got to her room, she went on Facebook and sent a message to Julie, her best college friend, who was in Florida for the vacation, about Dave. Her cell rang and it was Julie. "He said he found someone who looked like me, but was better than me."

"He said that?" Julie asked.

"Maybe I should have gone to Illinois." They talked and talked and finally Julie said she had to get to bed, that she would call in the morning. Katie got into bed thinking there must be something wrong with her. First, her mother gave her away, and then the person she thought she would marry tossed her aside like a used Kleenex.

After a restless few hours, Katie fell asleep and woke long after her parents had gone to work. The note on the kitchen table from her mom told her to call if she needed anything and that she'd be home around five thirty. Just as Katie felt tears starting again, her phone rang. Julie said she was ready to talk if Katie wanted to.

"Let me get a yogurt. I haven't eaten anything yet," Katie said.

After they talked for about an hour, analyzing all aspects of Katie and Dave's relationship, Julie said she had to go, that she would call again later. Katie washed out her yogurt cup and made some coffee. The house phone rang. When she said hello, her mother asked if she'd had breakfast yet. Katie told her she was making coffee and that she'd had some yogurt.

"How was your evening with Dave?"

"He broke up with me. He met someone he likes better."

"Oh, no. I'm so sorry, Katie. He seemed like a nice guy, but I guess you never know."

"I don't want to talk about it now. I have to go," Katie said.

"Okay, call me if you feel like it. See you tonight."

That night Katie and her parents talked. Her dad told her there were many fish in the sea. Katie excused herself and went up to her room. She and Julie talked for a long time.

Once classes started at the high school after New Year's Day, Katie decided to visit Mr. Rossa. "I'm glad to see you. How was it?" he asked. She told him her story, including the meeting with Allie and the breakup with Dave. He asked her to come back that afternoon to talk to his seniors about college life. Mr. Rossa always makes me feel better, she thought. When she returned after lunch to meet with his class, she was candid about the good and bad things she'd experienced, though she didn't add that she and her boyfriend had broken up. Katie ran into a couple of teachers in the hall who were happy to see her, and went home feeling good and energized about returning to Beacon.

Katie's second semester classes started. She liked English, music, and psychology, but had to struggle with biology. She told Ruth Ann about her plans to room with Julie next year.

"That's good. I'm hoping to room with Bonnie, a girl in my chem class."

"Can you believe how much has happened since we came last September," Katie said. "I never thought I'd meet someone who knew my birth mother. I'm glad I learned more about her, but it's not as important as I thought it would be."

The next day when they were having coffee, Julie asked if she wanted to go to a party Friday night. A few of her friends knew some guys who were in a fraternity that was having a scavenger hunt party on Friday.

Katie said she didn't know if she felt like it, but Julie insisted.

When Friday night came, Katie and Julie went with the group of other girls to the party. Katie didn't expect to have a good time, but to her surprise, she did. One of Julie's friend's, Linda, was also from Chicago and asked Katie if she was planning to go home for the summer. Katie said she probably would, but she needed to find a job and hadn't started looking yet.

"My dad owns a marketing company and he's looking for people to hire for the summer to work as interviewers for the surveys he does in shopping malls. I could give him your name if you want. I did it last year and it was fun and I made money."

Katie said she was interested and would send Linda her contact information. Well, Katie thought, if I can get that job, I'll be able to make some spending money. Maybe I should try to find a job in Boston. At least I wouldn't have to run into Dave. But, I have to save some money and living at home makes the most sense. Besides, my folks would be upset if I stayed here for the summer.

A few days later, Katie ran into one of the fraternity brothers in the gym. He was cuter than she remembered. They agreed to meet for a smoothie after they had finished their workouts.

Later that spring, Katie ran into Allie in the hall outside the Admissions Office. "Are you still interested in driving out to Laketon?"

Allie asked.

"I have a lot of work, but I would really like to go," Katie answered.

"Maybe we could do a quick trip and if you want to, go back when you have more time. It only takes about an hour to get there. We can be back within four hours." They talked about when to go and agreed on a Sunday in three weeks.

When the date arrived, Allie picked Katie up. On the drive out, they talked more about Paula. "I decided to see one of the counseling deans about her. Gail, the dean, has been helping me think about how I feel about Paula giving me up for adoption. Talking about it is helping. She thinks this trip is a good idea and also that I might want to meet Paula's mother someday."

Allie seemed surprised to hear this. "I could help you do that if you decide that's what you want to do. Mrs. Kotski has dementia, but from what I know, she still likes to see people." They talked about what Paula's family was like when Allie and Paula were in high school. When they got to Laketon, they drove first to the neighborhood where Paula had lived with her family. The house was pretty much the same as Allie remembered, though the paint was peeling and a basketball hoop was now in the driveway. They drove by the high school and other places that Allie said were important to Paula when she lived there including a pizza place where they had a quick lunch before driving back to Boston.

Allie felt emotionally exhausted after dropping Katie off at her dorm. Even though she was happy to get to know Katie, her memories of Paula were now affected by what she'd learned about Katie's feelings about being given up for adoption and how Paula had not told her birth father she was pregnant. Allie felt guilty about not remembering his name and not being that curious about him at the time. She wished she had learned more, but there was nothing she could do about that now.

———————

Back in her room, Katie told Ruth Ann about her day with Allie. When she finished, Ruth Ann told her about something that had happened when she was in her advisor's office a few days earlier.

"I was waiting for her to finish a phone call. I think she forgot I was there. Anyway I couldn't hear what she was talking about because I had earbuds in while I listened to my music. I'd just downloaded some new songs. The battery ran down and the music stopped. I heard Professor Dubrova say she thought the freshmen who got in through the lottery would be fine. She told the person she was talking to, to stop worrying. I thought that was kind of interesting, even though I didn't have any idea what she was talking about. She looked up and saw me looking at her so I started humming like I was listening to my music. She kept talking, but I didn't hear anything else interesting. I was going to take out my earbuds, when there was a knock on the door. This woman came in and didn't see me because I was sort of sitting behind the door, and she said 'I have the results for the freshmen that you wanted.' Professor Dubrova waived her hand at her and pointed at the phone and me. The woman turned around, saw me, and said, 'Oops, I'll come back later' before she closed the door. I heard Professor Dubrova say to the person on the phone that she'd call back later. She hung up and didn't say anything about the conversation. We talked a little about my courses for next fall, she signed my registration forms, and I left."

"Do you think your advisor is doing some kind of research on our class?" Katie asked.

"I don't know. Let's look at her website. She does research on the Pygmalion effect. If someone thinks they are expected to do well, they will do better than if they don't think they are expected to do well. Do you think we're in some kind of experiment?"

"I don't know. I can't think of anything unusual that's happened," Katie said.

"Why don't I post something on Facebook and ask if anyone knows anything about the Pygmalion effect and research and a lottery with the freshman class?" Ruth Ann said.

One respondent commented that if the freshmen accepted by lottery do not do as well as the other freshmen, the Admissions Dean should lose his job. Others responded that they thought they had been admitted by lottery because they didn't think they fit in.

Ruth Ann told Katie that Mike, the grandson of one of the trustees, a member of the freshman class, and Ruth Ann's boyfriend, read her question about a lottery, then emailed his grandfather to ask if he knew anything. His grandfather was surprised by the question and couldn't imagine anything like that happening at Beacon. He called Chuck Skinner who acted surprised, said he'd ask around, and get back to him. Ruth Ann said Mike thought the president would call the Dean of Admissions.

CHAPTER TWENTY

"**I** think we might have a problem with your experiment," Chuck said. He explained about the telephone call from the trustee. "If those admitted through the lottery don't do as well as the others, I don't think I'll be able to contain the uproar."

They both knew that after the first semester the randomly admitted freshmen had achieved lower grades than their counterparts. When the call ended, Max telephoned a recruiter who had contacted him earlier in the week to ask if he might be interested in a Dean of Admission and Financial Services position at Caltech. Max told him he'd changed his mind and he would be interested in finding out more about the position.

At home that night, he told Darleen what had happened and that he felt the lotteried-in freshmen would do fine this semester, but just in case they didn't he was going to cover his bases and interview for a position at Caltech. After the initial shock, she decided being closer to the twins who enjoyed being at college in California and seemed unlikely to return to the cold Northeast, would be a good thing. Max spent a long weekend in California interviewing for the position. A week later he was offered it and given another week to decide.

In the meantime, the semester ended and Sue finished the analysis of the grades of freshmen for the second semester. The results showed that the two groups of freshmen performed about the same in the second semester. There was no statistical difference. Marina's Pygmalion theory was supported, but it took two semesters not the one that Marina had expected and that Max had assumed.

A trustees' meeting was scheduled for the following week. Max was asked to be present for part of it. At the meeting, Mike's grandfather explained what he'd heard about a lottery. He asked Max whether there was an experiment involving the freshman class.

"I'm always interested in using research to inform the admissions process," Max said. "Professor Dubrova, a faculty member in the psychology department, and ˙I found our interests coincided. We selected four hundred of the two thousand freshmen to admit differently. We chose the four hundred from those who were academically equal to those admitted the traditional way and who were triaged in for a full read, but we didn't do the read and selected four hundred of that group randomly. In other words, we didn't read their essays or pay a lot of attention to their extracurriculars. We expected a fifty percent yield and we actually got a fifty-three percent yield. Professor Dubrova believed that the experimental group would do as well as those admitted the traditional way. I've just learned that after the spring semester the grades for both groups are not different. We feel the results support the notion of Professor Dubrova's theories." Max did not mention the higher proportion of those selected from the lottery who talked to the freshman dean's office about transferring to another college. Besides, they would not know until next fall whether those who talked about transferring actually followed through.

Some trustees huffed and puffed about putting Beacon's reputation at risk while others seemed intrigued by the experimental nature of the project. President Skinner admitted that he had allowed the experiment, but only for the relatively small number. By the end of the meeting, most of the trustees seemed more at ease with the experiment though a few felt that Max had taken too large a risk with Beacon's reputation. Max knew he would have to be extra vigilant in the next year to avoid raising any more questions in the minds of the trustees. He would be on the lookout for interesting positions elsewhere, although he didn't feel he had to leave right now. He turned down Caltech's offer.

The following September, Max and Marina sat

in his office listening to Sue go over the results of her data analyses comparing the percentage of special admits with the percentage of regular admits who had not returned for their sophomore year. Max and Marina knew last June that the special admits had visited the dean to discuss transferring to another college more often than the traditionally admitted group. Today's results were statistically significant with a higher proportion of special admits not returning, suggesting that the match was important. Even though the specials had done as well grade wise as the traditional admits by the end of their freshman year, apparently they were less enthusiastic about or comfortable with the Beacon culture. They thanked Sue for her work. "I'm going to meet a friend for lunch. Let me know if you need anything else," she said as she closed her backpack and headed toward the door.

"This is pretty interesting," Marina said. "I can get at least one publication out of it, maybe a book."

"If someone finds out and they weren't admitted the year we did the study, they'll think it was because of the lottery, and we'll have a public relations nightmare."

"I know. I'll have to think about that. Maybe I'll just write a novel," she joked. "What are you going to do in the future, now that you know how things worked out?"

"I'm not sure. We need to see what the total transfer out rate will be by the end of sophomore year. We were lucky that no reporter found out what we were doing. I wish there were some way we could do the lottery and not get into trouble, but I can't think of how. Finding out that the match has value, not so much for its relationship with grades but for our desire to enroll students who think this is the right college for them and want to stay until they graduate, is important."

"That's true. You would have to consider that aspect and see if you can refine who gets into the lottery pool."

"If we can accomplish that, then maybe there's some piece of the random experiment we can keep and use. I'm going to set up a meeting with Skinner and let him know how it all turned out. Without his support we couldn't have done it."

"I'm leaving because I have to teach at two thirty. I'll think about the best and safest way to write up the results of the experiment and be in touch."

After Marina left, Max's phone rang. A headhunter asked if he would like to interview for a position as vice president of enrollment management at a university in the Midwest. The job was at a higher level than his current one, paid more, and there might be a position at the university hospital for Darleen.

Typically, Max could imagine nothing better than making more money. Right now, though, he didn't think he wanted to leave, at least not yet. Darleen liked her job. The experiment had been interesting, had added some real drama to the soap opera trivialities that took place in the Admissions Office. He'd found the whole thing pretty exciting. In addition, at least for another year, Skinner would still be president and he was supportive. He'd heard about another book that disputed the value of timing the stock market. He was thinking of placing his retirement money in low fee and low load index funds and trying to ignore how they were doing at least on a daily basis.

Later, Max met with staff who knew about the special admit program. "You've heard that we're not going to use the lottery system next year. The randomly admitted freshmen did as well as the others, but they also more often talked with the dean about transferring out. Now, we've learned that a small though significantly higher proportion of special admits followed through and transferred to other colleges."

"I guess that means the match we talk about is important," Maggie said.

Max called to make an appointment to see President Skinner. He was told to come right over. As he walked, he reviewed the changes he'd made in the past few months: he went to the gym a few times a week where he'd become friends with the fellow who had the locker near his who worked in the law school. He felt less tense. His brother still made a lot more money than he did and could afford more things, but he and Darleen had enough money and they didn't need more things. The twins would be through with college soon and their finances would be better then.

When Max entered the president's outer office, the receptionist glanced up, said hello, and offered him a cup of coffee. He declined. He was still arranging the words in his head that he would say and didn't feel he could do that and drink coffee too. A few minutes later, Marti came out and invited Max to follow her inside. "How's it going?" She motioned for him to go into Chuck Skinner's office, where the president was on the phone.

Max took a seat on the other side of the desk, as Chuck waved hello to him and continued with the telephone call for another couple of minutes. Max busied himself with one of the magazines on an adjoining table. He glanced an at article about how a professor in the business school thought that trying to time the stock market was not only a waste of time but also a bad strategy. He was just getting into it when Chuck finished the phone call.

"So, have you and Marina had a chance to look at the transfer out data from the admissions experiment?" President Skinner asked.

"I'm here to give you a quick overview of what we found."

"Nothing bad, I hope?"

"As you know, when we compared the freshman second semester grades for those admitted through the lottery with those admitted the traditional way, we found no difference, and as you also know, the special admits more frequently talked with the dean about transferring out of Beacon. We now know that a small, though higher proportion of the specials followed through. That reinforces the belief that admissions people have about the need to find the match between the applicant and the college."

"At least their grades didn't suffer. But we certainly don't want to lose more freshmen to other colleges than we usually do. What was the transfer out percentage for the lotteried-in group and for those admitted the traditional way?"

"It was three percent for the traditional admits and five percent for the lotteried-in group. We lost four extra students due to the lottery."

"I'm glad we only admitted a small proportion through the lottery."

The phone rang. President Skinner looked at the caller's number and said, "I have to take this. Do you mind waiting? Stay where you are, I won't be long."

Max reached for the magazine he'd started reading earlier. Even though he already knew that market timing wasn't good, it still fascinated him. Too bad this article hadn't come out when he'd begun his market investing.

"Sorry, Max, I had to take that call from the mayor. If I don't take her calls, she gets bent out of shape. Now where were we—

more transferred out. Do you think there's any way of quickly assessing who has less of a match with our culture without doing a full second read?"

"Not right away, but my staff and I will continue to think about it."

"I'm glad we took the chance to do this. I hope Marina can avoid making everything too public. I'm sure she'll want to publish something."

"She's aware of the issues and I'm sure she'll do the right thing." At least I hope she does, he thought.

"Keep me posted if there are any new developments."

When Max walked into the reception area in the admissions office, he acknowledged the friendly glances of the staff, entered his own space, shut the door, sat down at his desk, took out his thermos, and had a long drink of black coffee. I guess I've come a long way, he thought. I was right to do the experiment.

Later, Max told the staff he'd turned down an opportunity to interview for a position as Dean of Enrollment Management at another university. They looked surprised and pleased. Andy said, "I'm glad I don't have to get used to a new boss." Others agreed.

"How did that student whose mother you knew in high school do?" Priscilla asked Allie.

"She did okay, though there were the usual ups and downs," Allie said. "We drove out to Laketon last spring and I showed her where her mother grew up."

Max knew, even if he had decided to leave for a new job, that Allie would still crunch numbers, James would continue to obsess about minority recruitment, Natalie would be Natalie, and the admissions office would be pretty much the same. Applicants would apply, some would be admitted, and many of those would enroll. Peter Plank would continue to be a little skeptical about the admissions business, but in his new position, Dean of the School of Science, his focus would be elsewhere, at least that's what Max hoped. Every year there was a lot of change, and at the same time, not very much. Max's faith in the admissions process had been reinforced.

Was it worth the extra effort and anxiety connected with the experiment, Max wondered? The confrontation with the trustees had been one of the worst moments, even though they were okay with the experiment in the end. Another low point had been when Marina spilled the beans at that conference and Peter Plank, of all people, was a friend of the person she'd talked to. Would Max agree to work with her again if she had a new idea? Although he'd had some sleepless nights because of her, on the whole he thought that participating in the experiment had made his life more interesting and less routine.

"Maybe," Priscilla said, "we can use the lottery again sometime."

"Maybe." Max said.

About the Author

Bette Johnson was Associate Director of Admissions for twenty-one years at the Massachusetts Institute of Technology (MIT). She has a Ph.D. in Educational Research from Boston College, a Master's degree from Northwestern University, and a Bachelor's degree from Tufts University. She lives in Massachusetts, and is married to John Williamson, Professor of Sociology at Boston College. Admission Lottery contains vignettes from her experience as well as some imagined possibilities.

Suggestions from the author about applying to college:

Apply to your dream college.

Apply to other colleges where you are willing to go and that admit a higher percentage of applicants than your dream school does.

More expensive colleges are not necessarily better for you. Consider the loan debt you will have for each of the colleges to which you have been admitted.

Plan to make the most of the opportunities at the college where you enroll.